That Girl Who?
Loosely Based on A True Story

Saniyah Baker-Boatwright

Copyright © 2019 Saniyah Baker-Boatwright
All rights reserved.
ISBN: 9780578541624

I dedicate this book to every girl that feels as if she has to be perfect all the time, feels as if she's tired of being judged at every angle, feels as if she can't be comfortable in her own skin, feels as if she doesn't have a home to turn to, feels as if life keeps throwing stone after stone at her, feels as if she has to put up a front to hide her true self and feels as if she can't seem to find her purpose or her faith.

Acknowledgements

I would like to thank God first and foremost for giving me the strength, courage, and guidance to write this book. Thank you, mom, for being in the process with me every step of the way. Thank you to Lebron and Destinee for putting up with your big sis and pushing me to stay focused throughout the process. Thank you Demarius and Binki for being in my corner and believing in me. Thank you to De'Andre Brown for going through this process of editing with me and being very supportive of my work. I truly couldn't have done it without you. Thank you to Dai Baker, Owner of Dai Baker Creative Group, for bringing my book to life and being supportive throughout the process. Thank you, Achaia Murphy, for bringing the vision of my Author Logo and any other graphical visions I had in mind to life and being supportive throughout the process. Thank you, Abigail Shamburger, for being a very supportive friend and providing great feedback. Thank you, Vincent Thomas, for being a part of this process and making sure my look is on point. Thank you so much to my book mentor, Jessica LeAnn, for staying on me throughout the process. Thank you, TWeen Queen Empowering Sisterhood, for being the best group of sisters anyone could ever have and aspiring me to be the best Queen I can be throughout this whole process. Thank you for every supporter of #TeamNiyah that I may have not mentioned. I love you all very much!

Table of Contents

Acknowledgements 4
Ch1 Peaches and Cream 6
Ch2 No Bullet Shall Prosper 16
Ch3 "Big Girl Panties" 22
Ch4 A Storm is Nearing 31
Ch5 Back to Hell or Off to Heaven 83
Ch6 How "Green" Are You? 89
Ch7 Heart Wants What the Heart Wants 98
Ch8 Can you be my baby girl? 121
Ch 9 It's Either Now or Never 134
Ch10 Family Matters 145
Ch11 For Better or Worse 165
Final Thoughts 180
About the Author 184

Ch1 Peaches and Cream

"You think you know it all.

You must get a lot of money?

You don't do anything but kiss the teacher's ass.

You don't ever want to have fun?"

Anything but what I picture myself to be as. My name is Diana Baker-Boatwright. You can call me Na-Na. Everyone pictures me as this well put together girl who doesn't go through anything in life. But the truth is I go through things just like everyone else. My goofiness covers the sadness that I feel inside. The difference is I tend to hide my emotions better than others.

I was born in Detroit, Michigan, August 7, 1999, to my parents Rochelle Baker and Julius Boatwright. I was a loveable, sassy, cute and chunky baby, so I was told millions of times. I honestly thought the world was peaches and cream growing up because everything seemed so fun and full of adventure. I guess that's because I had a large family which means a lot of cousins to hang with! There was always somebody's house to go over. My mother told me that I always got what I wanted because I was spoiled, and I would run off to my father for everything. What can I say, I was a daddy's girl and the only child, which usually means you get everything you want, right? So, I thought. Until I found out that I had two other brothers on my father's side. At the time, I really didn't understand how. Any who, their names are Bryan and Travis. Bryan, the oldest, was very strong-minded and could draw like a pro. Travis, a year older than me, was more laid back and goofy. He would have me in tears with all the jokes he would come up with. Not to mention, all they wanted to do was play basketball, videogames, and wrestle all day. I never understood the point of wrestling. What is the point of getting all sweaty and then someone getting hurt? The best part was that they always looked out for me. It's like they were my personal bodyguard. No one looked my way or said anything negative because they were ready to go off at any moment.

On, December 8, 2003, my mother welcomed in a healthy baby boy named Larry into our lives. Larry was a special name to my mother because it was her father's name and she wanted to honor him after his passing. I remember his birth like it was yesterday. I was behind the curtains as my mother had contractions and I began whining, "Why are yawl hurting my mommy?" All she could do was laugh and try to calm me down from behind the curtains to deliver my brother's big head. He was so cute and chunky.

I would walk around the house with him, give him his bottle, and change his diapers as if I was his mother. I guess you can say I learned the responsibility of taking care of people at an early age. But that was the role that came with being a big sister, right? I remember eating his baby food, the yellow baby cereal in the blue tube. I believe it's called Puffs, but anyway it's my favorite to this day. Alright, no more kids I thought to myself one day. I mean two should be enough plus the two children my father had. But what's crazy is I don't remember seeing them as much as I should have or would have liked to. I enjoyed having another sibling on my mother's side because I had somebody to play with at any time. I remember as if it were yesterday the day my mother told me I was going to be a big sister.

Walking into the bathroom, I heard sobbing coming through. My mama had what looked like a white stick in her hand. I asked, "Mommy what's wrong?" She looked at me and hugged me saying that everything was okay, she's just happy. But for some reason, I wasn't buying it. I felt like it was something wrong and she didn't know how to tell me. She convinced me that she was alright, so I left it alone. I walked back into the room to find my brother sleeping peacefully in his crib. He stayed smiling in his sleep. Seeing him happy made me happy, but I really wanted to wake him up so bad. Whenever I was around him, I would say my name hoping he would repeat it, so I could rub it in my mom and dad faces. Eventually my mom told us that she was pregnant and that this time it was a girl. My last sibling conceived was my annoying younger sister, Bambino, on March 8, 2005. She came out of the womb crying and sneezing. There's nothing I wouldn't do for my brother or sister. I was both their bodyguard and best friend and their mother when I needed to put my foot down to show them who was in charge.

Shortly after my sister's birth, my mom made the decision that we were moving to Alabama. She was fed up with all the lying, cheating, and the going back and forth with my dad. He would lie about his whereabouts, go out and cheat with several women, and then come back as if nothing ever happened. It was breaking my mom's heart and pushing her further away. She and my grandmother also thought the neighborhood was getting a little rough and figured we would have a better life moving to the South. However, the biggest reason is because she wanted to make sure that her mother was moving on well after taking the death of her husband very hard. My grandmother's boyfriend, Bernard, helped us load our things onto his truck. He seemed cool, didn't really know him, but such words as "pops" and "grandpa" started growing on my brother, sister, and I. Not having the opportunity to meet my maternal grandfather, I felt the gap was closed when I met Bernard.

My father was angry that we were moving away. I could tell by the sound of his voice when they were on the phone. It made my mom second guess that she was doing the right thing. But then again, she wasn't getting the support and love she needed, so she figured, why stay. Arriving in Alabama was a fun and long trip because of the scenery. Along the way, we had to stop to make sure our baggage wasn't falling and check to see if the kids needed to be changed or not. When we arrived, it took some getting used to. I missed my dad, family, and friends that we left back in Michigan. There was no more walking up the street to Dairy Queen or going to the corner store to getting Better Made potato chips and Faygo pop. I had to get used to the environment around me, understand how they talked, and know the right places to be in. If you didn't say ma'am and sir when you addressed people, it was viewed as disrespectful. If you went to certain areas, you were viewed as poor. And words like strawberry were pronounced with a "c" instead of a "t". When I talked, it was seen as talking proper. And where I was from drinks were called pop, instead of soda. It was a huge adjustment to keep myself aligned with how things were running.

One day, I was about to open my grandmother's door and heard her speaking with my Aunt Wilcher, so I leaned against the crack of the door, eavesdropping on the conversation. The conversation went:

Grandma: "Everything's going good. I'm going to the market tomorrow to get some Greens. You want some?"

Aunt Wilcher: "Yeah, get me like three big bundles. How is the healing coming along?"

Grandma: "It's going good. I'm feeling a lot better and okay sis. Talk to you later. I'm about to take my medication."

Aunt Wilcher: "Okay, have a good day. Bye."

Hanging up the phone, grandma turned on the tv. I knocked on her door and waited for her to tell me if I could come in. She gave me the okay and I laid down on her bed. "Hey Pooh Pooh," she smiled. "Hey granny, what are you doing?" I asked her. "Just got off the phone with your Auntie Wilcher. When we go over there sometime this week, she's going to give us some fresh Greens." "Oh ok," I say yawning. Leaving her room, I went into my mother's room to see if she was up. She was on the phone talking to my father, but she looked stressed and overwhelmed. "Here you go," she said in a cracking voice, handing me the phone.

"Hey, daddy's baby, what are you doing?"

"Nothing just came in mama room. When are you going to move down here with us?"

"I don't know yet. We'll see. I miss you, baby."

"Okay. I'm about to go play with the videogame. I miss you too"

"All right give the phone back to your mama. I love you."

"Love you too."

I really wanted my parents together, but they couldn't seem to find a common ground. I felt very sad to not see us together as a family, especially seeing other kids with both of their parents. I really had hope that they would get back together, but they always seemed to have excuses as to why it might not work. I was confused as to where things were headed. At times, it felt like they had potential and other times it felt like a ship ready to sink at any moment. Passing my mother the phone, I returned to my room to see if my brother was up yet. Larry and Bambino woke up around the same time. We played videogames up until it was time to go to bed. A couple of days passed by and we went over my Aunt Wilcher's house. It was a decent wooden house filled with pictures throughout the living room. It was fun going over there because one thing everybody knew about my aunt is that she knew how to throw down in the kitchen and she had all the jokes. My favorite was her red velvet cake and pecan pie! Man, you're talking about somebody that put her big foot in her food, skip that she put the whole leg in there. "Tinker Bell" is the nickname she gave me. I always wondered how she came up with that name for me. I mean I liked Tinker Bell but, she wasn't my favorite.

Anyway, one day, she was babysitting her grandchild, Carga. She seemed very friendly and enthusiastic. She grabbed me by my hand and led me into her room, saying that we were going to go play. I looked around her room noticing a big bed, an old-fashioned television, and some Barbie dolls in the corner. I could hear my mother laughing so hard I thought the roof was going to cave in. I looked over at my cousin locking the door. In my mind, I thought, why is she locking the door. As if she knew what I was thinking, she looked at me and said, "They're getting too loud." Next thing I knew, she began pulling down my shorts. My heart started racing and my palms started sweating because I knew at this very moment things were about to take a turn for the worst. For some reason, I couldn't scream. I couldn't cry. I felt numb all over. All kinds of thoughts were racing through my mind---bad ones. It's like someone took my voice box leaving me to gasp for air. I knew what she was doing to me was wrong. But how could I stop her? If I told, what would happen to me?

She laid me on the floor and began to touch my breast, although I barely had any at the time. I began to pull up my shorts saying, "No, please stop." She looked at me as if she could see through my soul replying, "No, and if you tell you're going to get in trouble and my grandma is going to whoop you." Shaking my head, I laid there, while she licks down to my stomach. She goes down to my center licking while I remained as still as a corpse breathing steady breaths hoping that someone would come to save me. Thinking to myself, why me God? Why did you just let my cousin, "MY COUSIN", lock the door and rape me! Now, of course, she wants me to return the favor. So, she pulled her shorts down and grabbed my head and forced it to her center. I started to slob on her to make it seem as if I was actually doing something. My auntie yelled out, "Girls go feed the dogs for me."

Carga jumped faster than a K-9 sniffing for weed, zipped up her pants, and unlocked the door all in one motion. I wanted to act as if nothing ever happened, so I rushed over to the bathroom grabbed the orange bar of soap, rubbed it all over my hands and even put some in my mouth. Although I washed my hands and mouth, I still felt dirty. I could still feel her hovering over me, breathing the same air that I was breathing and staring at me as if I was her prize possession. Before I opened the door to head outside, my mom asked me if I was okay. I smiled slightly and told her, yeah. I was crying on the inside, trying to figure out a way to tell my mom. I couldn't think of anything at the moment. That's when I felt hands rubbing my butt. It was Carga again. Pushing her and telling her to stop, I tried to walk away. However, she said we had to finish playing our "game." By this time, we are behind the house and she is singing wedding songs. She pushed up on me and began grinding against me. While she had me leaned up against the house, she's stuck her hands in my shorts locating my hole and began to thrust her finger in and out. The innocent little girl I once was, was now gone! To make matters worse, she had already convinced my mom that I could stay the night. And guess what? This time no was going to mean no!

We got to her house and by then it was bedtime. We already had our pajamas on because we took a bath at my auntie's house. She had a bunk bed and we both climbed on top. She tried to put her hands in my pants, but I pulled her hands away from my clothes. After that, she gave me some candy and I begin to feel really sleepy and dozed off. Carga had a dominant personality and it scared me. My body and mind were so in shock it felt as if I didn't have the mind control to react. The best way to put it is I was NUMB. I knew, telling what happened wasn't going to be easy. Will anyone believe me? What if this is something that is acceptable in the family and I failed the test by telling someone? What if my mama kills Carga if she found out what she did to me? Will my mama kill me for allowing Carga to do that to me and not say anything? From that day forward, I decided that I would never bring it up. I would act as if it never happened. Months went by with the routine of coming from school to daycare, then home. Because my mom worked at the daycare, it made things a lot easier. One morning looking out the window, I saw a white van passing by slowly. Going into my room, I climbed on top of my bunk bed and reached for my diary. I ran across the letter that I had written to my mom explaining what Carga did to me. Tearing out the page, I threw it to the floor hoping that my mom would come in and notice it enough to pick it up. Just like clock-work, my mom came into the room. "What are you doing in here, Pooh? And clean this room up, she said. "Can't be living like no pig now." "Help me clean up my room," I giggled. "Nope, you are a big girl, you got it." I thought to myself, I'm not going to ever be able to tell her. I cleaned up the room and threw the paper away. On the other hand, my mind was just like focus on passing the fifth grade and everything would be okay.

Ch2 No Bullet Shall Prosper

In the middle of archery practice, our coach blew the whistle and told us to slowly put our bows down. I slowly pushed back the bowstring to its original form and looked over at my coach. "Diana, you have an early dismissal," she said looking in my direction. I put my bow and arrow away, got my bookbag, and headed for the door. Behind the door was my grandmother and Uncle Chris. What could be so important that they pulled me from my archery practice? I asked myself. I mean everybody knew how I felt about archery. Archery was life. I loved the feeling of the bow and arrow in my hand.

My uncle grabbed one hand and my grandmother grabbed the other, walking me to the car. "What's wrong? Why yawl looking like that?" I asked. Grandma replied, "Your mother was almost killed. We're on our way back to the house to figure out what we're going to do". I completely blacked out after that. I remember my eyes shutting and them tapping me to wake up. Pulling up to the house, I wake up and see familiar cars in the yard. All of us get out of the car and walk into the house. Rushing over to my mom, I asked, what happened? With tears in her eyes, she explains, "I picked your brother and sister up from school and when arriving at the house my intuition told me to keep the car in park. The screen-door was ajar, but I didn't think anything of it because it was windy, and you know how the screen-door acts up. I saw a figure at the door and yelled, what the fuck are you doing in my house? The white man held a gun to my forehead. Pop! He shot the gun, but no bullet came out. I don't know what came over me, but I slammed the door and hopped back into the car putting it in reverse.

The man came out behind me, running after the car, and steadily tried to shoot the gun. I yelled to the kids, stay low to the floor of the car! They were crying, shaking, and peeing uncontrollably. Shaking, trying to get away from the scene, I noticed an undercover cop and pulled over. The cop waved his hand, signaling me to drive to the other side. He turned on his sirens and headed in the opposite direction of me. So now we're waiting to hear back from the police station to see where we go from here." Wiping her face, I hugged her and told her that I was glad nothing happened to her and that I loved her. The familiar cars that I saw in the driveway belonged to my uncles or their girlfriend. I went over to my brother and sister and held them in my lap. Everybody was talking at once and I blurted out that I didn't want to live there anymore, and we should move somewhere else. I started crying and Bernard said that someone should give me some medicine so I can calm down. In the end, we came up with the decision that we would stay with my mom's best friend Keisha for the time being. So, we packed some of our items and spent two weeks living with Keisha.

Keisha welcomed us in her home and made us feel comfortable. Within a week, one of the officers on the case called my mom and said, "The man who attacked her has been watching our home for days, if not longer, from his white van, because we were "flashing". And the man that just so happened to be sitting on the corner was a detective that was working on a case at the end of the block." After finding his I.D in the area, they eventually caught the man and sentenced him to 10 years in prison. From that day forward, I was so terrified of white vans because it made me wary of who was in them. I prayed to God and thanked him for saving my mother. I knew I was going to go crazy if I came home that day and she wasn't there.

Eventually, we moved back into our house and obtained an alarm system. Bernard came over and boarded the front door and made sure the windows were secured. Months went by and everyone started to feel better about the situation. It was a struggle to not re-live that event, but with the support of one another, we pulled through. The next morning, I woke up from a good sleep and found my way stumbling to the bathroom. Looking down in the toilet, I notice that it was something red mixed in with my pee. "Mama come here. I think I'm bleeding," I yell. She came into the bathroom looking all around me. She asked, "Where?" I pointed to the inside of the toilet bowl and she told me to wipe. I did as she said, and Lord beholds its blood on the tissue. "Man, I don't want this. Can we go to the doctor to get this stopped?" I whine. "Nope. Welcome to womanhood my love," said my mother. "Take a shower and I'll fix you some hot tea." Stripping from my clothes, I stepped into the tub and pulled the curtain shut. I lathered up my body and rinsed off. Next, I picked out a dark-colored towel from the closet and dried off. My mom knocked on the door and asked if I need help putting it on. "Nope, I know how to do it," I told her.

Next thing I knew, she called my aunts to tell them I have my period now. I thought to myself like dang everybody ain't got to know. What's so important about it anyway? My aunts were on the phone crying as if somebody died. I started laughing because it really wasn't that serious. Walking into the room, I laid in bed, sipped my tea, and watched TV. My stomach began cramping so I went to sleep. About 30 minutes later, I woke up and walked into the livingroom. "Why is the furniture wrapped up?" I ask as my mother as she walked past me. "I don't know, your grandmother did it," she replies as she entered her bedroom. I felt like the only reason she did that was because she felt like I would probably get blood on the furniture. My brother and sister were asleep, so I went with my mom and we watched Martin. The next day I woke up and did not want to go to school. My mom and grandmother walked me to class to speak with my teacher about me being on my period. "I got her. She'll be just fine," my teacher patted me on the shoulder. Walking slowly into the classroom, I took my seat feeling as if all eyes were on me or maybe it was me being paranoid, wondering if people could tell if I was on my period. The day went well until I sneezed. I didn't know whether to laugh or cry because of the feeling I felt underneath.

    I raised my hand to go to the bathroom. I walked inside the bathroom stall and sat my purse on top of the tissue rack. Riiiip! I hated the noise the wrapper made when taking the pad out. I finished my business and grabbed my purse. "You're on your period, huh?" Some girl asked me. "Wow, it's that noticeable," I replied. "No, I just figured because you had a purse now and I saw your people this morning at the door. It's okay, I have mine too. If you ever need a pad, let me know." She said. I smiled, washed my hands, and returned back to the classroom. It felt good to know that someone understood what I was going through. Later that day, the bell rang, and I walked down to the carpool area. I arrived home and took a shower. Just as I was done putting on clothes, my mom came through the door. "You need any help with homework?" she asked.

"Nope, I got it," I said. "But you can sharpen my pencils for me." Pulling out the pencils from my pouch, she raised up two of the smallest pencils saying, "even these little nubs? You should throw these away." "But they still write the same, mama," I laughed.

I was getting ready to go in the kitchen and a car was in the driveway. Knock! Knock! Already knowing who it is, I yelled out, "Who is it?" anyways. "Your Uncle Chris," he yells back. I opened the door and he gave me a hug. My grandmother came from the back and sat down on the couch in the living room. "Yawl come outside. I got a surprise for yawl." Chris laughed. My brother, sister, and I ran behind him and he opened up his back door and out came a white and black dog. My sister and brother ran back into the house. "Granny and mama, can we have him please?" I begged. "Who's going take care of it?" they asked at the same time. "Me!" I exclaimed. I rubbed his head, thinking of a name. Yelling out loud, "I'm going to name him Beast". Chris chained him up to the tree in the backyard and sat a bucket of water by him and a kennel of food. He gave us a bag of dog food and we sat it on the floor at the bottom of the pantry. "Wash your hands," grandma said to me while I was coming in the house. "All right, family, I'm gone," Uncle Chris said getting into his car. I peeped out the window to see Beast peeing on the tree. He was an obedient dog. I couldn't wait to go shopping for toys and other doggy items. Teaching him tricks and going to the park was also on my to-do-list. I grabbed some yogurt from the refrigerator and went to finish my homework.

Reminiscing about being back in my hometown, I picked up my Cabbage Patch Doll and played with her hair. I wished my dad would come down and live with us. But it seemed like every time we talked about it; he would go around the conversation. Maybe one day we'll be a family again, I thought to myself. My brother came into the room, interrupting my thoughts to tell me to come here. I followed him to our mother's room and there was a movie on the screen. He cracked up laughing and I laid down on the bed. A week later was my 5th-grade graduation. That day I came out on top, bringing home countless awards from 'A' Honor Roll to the Woodmen of the World Award. My mom had balloons in the car and wrote Congratulations on the car, tooting her horn all the way to the house, while I waved my hand like a Queen. Changing out of my clothes after taking countless pictures, I went outside and played with my brother and sister. My mom had the door open watching us while frying chicken. My grandmother pulled over onto the grass since we were playing in the driveway. She came out with a gift bag in her hand walking towards me. "Sorry for missing your graduation," she hugged me. I thanked her and went inside the house to show my mom what she got me. My grandmother told everybody to meet in the living room. "I have great news. I found a house. We're moving!" she smiled. I was glad we were moving because I didn't want to go to the school down the street. I heard negative things about the school and didn't want to be put in that environment.

Ch3 "Big Girl Panties"

I had a wonderful time during my elementary school years and made countless memories. I wish I could have stayed, but I knew it was time to move on to bigger and better things. It was time to put on my "big girl panties". During the first day of 6th grade, it was chaotic getting everybody from class to class. Some of my peers asked me questions like, "why do you have two last names, do you have a lot of money, is your mom or dad white or do you have a boyfriend?" It was during this time I wished I had an older sibling or cousin that went to school with me, so I could feel more comfortable. One day I came home and told my mother and grandmother about my day and with a cup of hot cocoa and marshmallows they made me feel better about the days ahead.

Within weeks, I dreaded coming to Greensville Middle School. Every other day if someone wasn't trying to start a fight with me, someone was talking behind my back or to my face. I couldn't grasp why there was so much hatred towards me or why everyone tried to pick a fight with me. I simply wanted to mind my own business and get along with everyone. Many days I cried and prayed myself to sleep and hoped everything would get better. The next morning, I showered and got ready for school. My grandmother dropped me off at school because my mother had to work. I walked into my homeroom class and sat in my assigned seat. The teacher sat at the desk and called roll while we were working on the Bellringer. Minutes later we switched over to the next class. We settled in and waited for the teacher to instruct us on what we were going to do. She then gave us instructions and walked out of the classroom to go to the restroom. "Aye, show Diana, I bet she doesn't know anything about that," some kid yelled from across the room.

I looked to the side of me and a boy came over to sit by me. He waved his phone across my face. The phone showed a naked man and woman having sex. My face went blank; he laughed hysterically and returned to his seat. After the strange encounter, I went back to talking to my friend and asked, what was that? "It was porn," she said and questioned why I had never seen it before. I laughed and went on with the rest of the school day. I arrived at my home and of all the questions to ask my mother, for sure it wouldn't be about porn. I came into the kitchen to get a snack and Bernard was sitting on the barstool. "How are you doing and how are things at school?" he asked. "Everything is going well, but I'm still adjusting," I answered. He then began to ask questions about my cousin Ashley. I told him that she's doing well. Next, we began talking about a situation at school and he said to me "you should be more like Ashley". Irritated by his remark, I said yeah okay and went to tell my mother what he said. Shaking her head, she told me not to let what he said get to me and that I should keep being the same beautiful and unique person I am. Feeling better about the situation, I told her that I was going to bed and went into my room. Turning off the TV, I slid underneath the covers and set my alarm.

Knock! Knock! My mother came through the door and told me to start getting ready for school so she could drop us off. Stretching and yawning, I grabbed my uniform and underclothes and brought them to the bathroom with me. I showered, put lotion on, and then my clothes. Everybody was dressed and heading to the car. I hopped in the front seat and turned on the radio. I loved listening to the Steve Harvey Morning Show and Nephew Tommy's prank calls. After hearing to the ending, I got out of the car and went to the front office to say the morning announcements. Next, I walked to my math class. As I sat down, a girl sitting behind me tapped my shoulder. I turned to see what she wanted. "Is your name Diana Baker-Boatwright?" she asked. Weirdly looking at her, I replied, yes. Did you know that you're online, she asked, showing me a picture on her phone? Yes, I knew that I said while turning around in my seat. I thought to myself, who makes time out of their day to look up somebody in the middle of class? The bell rang and that was my cue to go to my keyboarding class.

The keyboarding teacher passed around the papers with the objective for the day. I sat in the back of the class, so I received the last of the papers. I raised my hand and explained to the teacher that there were extra papers. She looked at me and gave a fake smile, saying, "you know you are really different. I don't know why you act so different." I thought to myself, all this drama because I tried to give her back the additional copies. Avoiding confrontation with her, I gave the copies to another student to pass up to her. Then, it seemed as if she was trying hard to press her nasty attitude on me. Fed up, I walked out of the class to go to the office. I waited for someone to assist me and said, "I want someone to call my mother to the school." My mother and grandmother came together. The assistant principal addressed the situation and my family took me home. Every other day if it wasn't someone trying to start a fight with me, it was someone talking behind my back or to my face. I couldn't understand why there was so much hate towards me. I looked in the closet and saw that there was a hanger without a piece of clothing hanging on it. I grabbed it and started to place it over my head. It wouldn't fit. I heard someone pass by and threw the hanger back into the closet. I then slumped down in the closet and began sobbing silently.

During my eighth-grade year, I joined the basketball team. People started to be a little nicer to me, but I would still have bad days here and there. I told myself, at least it's not as bad as it used to be. It was time for practice and our coach was not there yet, but we knew we had to stretch. Therefore, our team captain led us into our stretches. Out of nowhere, a rat scurried across the floor near the captain and everybody ran. The coach came through the door asking, "why are you all running?" We told her, she laughed and started roll call. We got into our drills and ran some plays. Afterward, we were all tired and went to get water. After coming back, we talked to the coach for a moment and everybody called their ride to go home. Instantly, I saw my ride as I got ready to exit the door. I slid in the car, body sore from practice, and turned on the air conditioner.

The next day came and my alarm didn't go off, so I rushed to get ready. I tapped on my mother's door and everybody hurried to get dress. Luckily, the school was somewhat up the street and I was only a few minutes late. I got a pass from the office and quickly went to my homeroom class. We sat there for some time and then we went to the computer lab. It was "Pace Day" for me, so I waited to see if Mrs. Thompson was going to pop in on us. As soon as I thought about it, she came around the corner. A select few of us walked down to our Pace class and sat in our assigned seats. Mrs. Thompson started to describe the project that was due in three weeks. She then left the room to go run off some copies. As soon as she left, the topic of discussion was me. Miranda said, "We feel like you don't like to have fun and you act stuck up all the time." Then, Dejah said, "You act like you are better than everybody and you walk like you have a stick stuck up your butt." Then, Lauryn came over by me and said, "Yeah we are not trying to be mean, but it's true and that's how we see it." All I could do was cry because I was baffled as to why I was receiving all this hate. That's when my teacher returned to the classroom and rushed over to me and asked, "What's going on?" The bell rang and the teacher told everybody to go to their next period and asked me to stay behind.

I walked to the library with streams of tears running down my face. The librarian, whom I happened to be very close to, asked me what was wrong and if I wanted to talk about it. She pulled me into her office and closed the door. I held my hands to my face not wanting to be seen crying. She tried to pry my hands away and to get me to talk. I told her about the situation that occurred, and she began to console me and handed me a tissue. She then pats me on the back and explained, "sometimes people are jealous of you, and you cannot let their opinions affect how you view yourself." At that moment, I learned that people's opinion about me was just that, an opinion, and nothing I should worry about. I could no longer show weakness and let the words of others affect me. Sure, words hurt, but they are just words. She told me to return to class and that she would handle it. I returned to class with a stronger attitude, understanding that people's words held no power over my life and deserved zero of my energy.

Having a rough time at Greensville Middle School, I knew I needed to stand up for myself. I could not continue to let bullies overpower me. The bell rang for the car riders to report to the front of the building. I grabbed my book bag and left the classroom. I got in the car and my mother asked, how was your day? We talked about the situation that happened at school, and I assured her that I could handle it. Of course, she asked me if she needed to come to the school and again, I explained that I could handle it. We got home and I saw she cooked my favorite, seafood! I quickly washed my hands and started fixing my brother, sister, and I a plate. I sat at the barstool and started peeling my shrimp. Sitting there for about fifteen minutes, I was stuffed and got up to put my dishes in the sink. I grabbed my book bag out the corner and pulled out my folder to complete my homework. I was done within ten minutes and went to shower. Getting out the shower, I went to my room to watch TV and fell asleep.

The next morning the smell of food tickled my nose and I quickly got out of bed. Rubbing my eyes, I walked into the kitchen to see my mother cooking breakfast. "Go wake your brother and sister and tell them to come and eat," she instructed. I quickly went to wake them and returned to the kitchen. She sat beside me and ate with us. I sipped the last bit of orange juice and went to get ready for school. My mom dropped me off at school and I went to my first-period class, sat down, and took out my binder. The day moved pretty fast. It seemed like every time I looked up it was time to move to the next class. Our science teacher walked us down to the gym and sat down on the bleachers. We had the option of playing basketball or staying in the bleachers. I decided to go shoot around to kill time. Kailyn passed me the ball and I shot it from the three-point line. Wham! A ball came out of nowhere and hit me on the side of my head. Losing consciousness and seeing nothing but darkness, I slowly dragged myself over to my P.E teacher, Mrs. Myers and slumped over into her arms.

Another student helped carry me to the office. Tears ran down my face and I could barely talk. "Call my mother," was the only thing I could manage to get out. My mother and grandmother arrived and immediately began asking questions about what happened. We hurried out of the school and my grandmother drove with the emergency lights on. I cried so hard that my grandmother pulled the car over and asked what was wrong. Through my sobs, I told her that my face was burning and my head hurting. They called the police and told them about the situation. The ambulance arrived in no time. My mom got out of the car and helped me onto the stretcher. While in the ambulance, they notice my breathing was sketchy and put a mask over my face to help me get more oxygen. We arrived at Mount Sanai Hospital and they help me onto the bed. The nurse came in to check my pulse, temperature, and other vital signs. "I'll get you some Powerade so you can hydrate," she said. I laid in the bed as my mother and grandmother told me jokes in an attempt to cheer me up. I was angry because I didn't know who threw the ball or why they threw it so hard. The doctor came in and told me that I had a mild concussion and to make sure that I stayed hydrated. We left the hospital in time enough to go pick up my brother and sister. Pulling up to McDonald's, we ordered food to take home. We went into the kitchen and ate our food. Next, everybody took their showers and went to chill in their room. I was exhausted, so I went and got in bed with my mother and went to sleep.

It seemed like time after time I was back and forth and in and out of the hospital because I kept passing out or having seizures.

That next day we had a meeting at the school about the ball being thrown at my head and the administrators claimed the cameras weren't clear enough and nobody knew who threw the ball. Different students were asking me if I knew who threw it and it was nerve-wracking to the point I just wanted to go home. I slept and ate through the end of my eighth grade. I couldn't wait to leave school and never look back. To pass time, I did a countdown of how many days I had left. It worked, and now it was graduation day. My mom dropped me off at school while everybody else finished getting ready at the house. I wore a white dress that my grandmother made for me, light make-up, and hair bone-straight. Everybody I encountered told me how precious I looked. Minutes passed and now we were walking into the back doors of the gym. We sat down in our positioned seat and waited for all the family to arrive before starting the program. Gazing through the crowd, I looked for my family in the stands. Suddenly, I spotted my sister and brother waving at me. Smiling, I waved back and focused back towards the program. The principal said his remarks and then it was time for names to be called. Rows and rows of names were called and then they finally called mine, "Diana Baker-Boatwright." I heard my family cheering for me in the stands, making embarrassing noises. Then, my Uncle James came up to me with his camera, I stopped and posed to take pictures. I heard somebody in the audience say, "dang that girl racking up all of the awards." About an hour after the conclusion of the ceremony, I found my family in the back of the school. Everybody hugged and congratulated me on moving on to high school. We got in our cars and a bird flew by the school. I told the bird, "Fly away as fast as you can and don't look back. Whatever you do, don't stop at this school." Laughing all the way home, we pulled up to the house and I began reminiscing about all the good and bad memories from Greensville Middle School. Going through life, you see everything for what it is. Things aren't always peaches and cream, but it's up to you to advocate for yourself. I learned that I didn't have to blame myself for the actions of others.

Ch4 A Storm is Nearing

Grabbing my pajamas out of the dresser, I went into the bathroom and closed the door. I plugged up the radio that was sitting by the sink. Stepping out of my clothes and grabbing a washcloth, I lathered up the Dove soap and began to wash my body. My mom came through the door and started putting conditioner in her hair. Next thing you know, the whole room turned black and I could feel my body dashing through the curtain. Seconds later, my hearing started coming back and I heard, "Bring her some clothes." "What's going on? What happened?" I asked confusedly, trying to raise my head up, but it felt heavy and as if someone's body was beneath me. My mom was holding me, as I was lifting up. Covering me in a towel, she pulled me up and walked me over to the couch to lay me down. My sister was crying trying to figure out what was going on with me. My brother passed my mama some clothes and she helped me put them on. Knock! Knock! My grandmother went to open the door and the paramedics came rushing over to me to check my vitals and asked me some questions. Two paramedics came through the door with the stretcher and placed me on top of it. The family followed behind the paramedics to the hospital.

I was kind of going in and out of it while the paramedics were trying to keep me alert. Getting me in the back room, I was told to relax as they were putting an I.V. in me to give me medications to ease the pain. My family was gathered in the room sitting along the side in the chairs. Dr. Bonds came in and asked, "So, what's going on today?"

Mom: "I was conditioning my hair and all of a sudden, I see the imprint of Diana body coming towards me crashing through the curtain. Before she could fall to the floor, I stopped what I was doing and caught her. I was calling her name, but she wasn't responding. That's when her eyes rolled to the back of her head, face turned pale, lips turned blue, and it looked as if she took her last breath. While holding her in my arms and yelling to call 911, her body started shaking."

Dr. Bonds: "So, it appears as if she had a seizure and from the tests we ran, it seems she is a bit dehydrated. We will keep her for a little bit to make sure she's okay. Also, we want to make sure there wasn't any damage done to her brain, so I will have my nurse take her to get a CT Scan. I know this seems quite scary, but it's just a machine that we use to examine the brain. Nothing to worry about, she will be okay, mom."

Mom: "Okay, when will we get the results back? Should I follow up with her personal doctor?"

Dr. Bonds: "You will get the results back today and yes, I do recommend you doing that."

A nurse came in and gave me a cup of Gatorade and it tasted terrible. I hurried and swallowed, pinching my nose. She told me it would help get me rehydrated. My family laughed at me chugging the drink back. In walked the nurse with a clipboard and a wheelchair and said, "Alright, mom we're going to take her to the back for the CT Scan." My mom replied, "Can I come too?" "Yes, you may," she smiled. The nice lady rolled me out the door with my mother following right behind us. The lady helped me onto the laid-out bed with the overhead connected to it. Slowly the machine moved me forward and red lights were circling the machine and I moved my head to see what was going on. "Be still sweet pea," the nurse said, "The red light won't hurt you. It's detecting anything that's going on with your brain." I closed my eyes and stayed as still as I could be. Then, the machine pulled me away out towards the opening. My mom and the nurse came over to assist me back to the wheelchair. She strolled me back to my room and helped me back onto the bed, as I was still a little dizzy. My siblings and grandma were making jokes to cheer me up.

A couple of minutes later, the doctor went over what I needed to do and the results from my CT Scan. "Everything looks fine. The results showed no damage to the brain. So, you are cleared to go," the doctor said. "But we have prescribed some pills for the pain." He handed my mom some papers to sign and we were on our way out the doors. Grandma Mary drove to CVS so I could pick up my medicine. We walked into the store and picked up the prescription, which was ready upon arrival. Walking outside, darkness fell upon us. No one felt like cooking, so we picked up some McDonalds before pulling up at the house. Everybody showered and got into their pajamas after eating. Unfortunately, I had to take a supervised bath due to the doctor's orders. To give me my privacy, my mom gave me a bell to ring in case of an emergency and she left the door open, so she could hear if anything went on. I walked into my mom's room to take my medicine and then, back to my room to fall asleep.

Just like that summertime had gone by before we knew it. Sure enough within the blink of an eye, ninth grade came around like a thief in the night. Being in high school was starting off as a great experience. I wasn't being bullied, I didn't care about what people thought of me, and I was actually getting acquainted with friends and clubs. However, I would have episodes of seizures every now and then. Besides that, I made a friend, Viola, who was very smart and had a kindhearted spirit. "Hey girl," she said. I walked by her on my way to my next class going out the door, heading into the next building. Our high school was like a college campus, but I loved it. I finally made it to my next class right before the late bell rung. "Alright class, you can take out your notebook," Mrs. Murphy said. Everybody did what they were told, while she took roll. After a while, a movie was put on and a worksheet was passed out to answer questions as we went along. An hour into class passed by and the lights were cut back on. We put our worksheet in our binder to go over the answers in class the following day. It was finally time to go home.

Walking into the house, I put my book bag by the door. I went into the kitchen, washed my hands, and got a snack. I didn't have any homework because I had already done it while I was at school. Eating on some fruit cocktail, I went into my room and turned on the TV. I peeped out the window to see if Beast was outside. Normally, he could sense I was in my room and would come put his paws on my window. I got up to feed him and make sure he had water in his bucket. "Beastie, Beast!" I yelled out over and over again. But I didn't see him anywhere nor did I hear any barking. I went out the front door to see if he was on the other side of the gate. He was nowhere in sight. I started to panic and by this time I began looking to see if there were any signs of him escaping from the gate. I ran back into the house and out the back door. "He's right here," my grandmother said. "He's dead". I was so numb that I couldn't even move anything but my mouth was wide open. All I could feel were the tears rolling down my face. "No," I yelled out. "When I checked on him this morning, he was fine. He was playing with his toys." Beast was my best friend, protector, and most of all the one who listened to my cries. It hurt so much to see him like that.

He laid there, lifeless, eyes grey as a beautiful storm, and tongue sticking out like a withered plant. All the memories we had together started flooding my mind. I went back into the house thinking that it had to be a bad dream that I couldn't wake from. My sister and brother were sitting over on the couch crying, as my mother consoled them. "Can we bury the dog, mom?" I asked. From outside the back door, my grandma yelled, "You all are going to have to move this dog." Walking past her, I looked over to see she was on the phone laughing. She didn't show any remorse for us losing Beast. I was so disgusted by the way she was acting, as it's "just a dog". We came outside to see blue tarp in my grandmother's hand. She placed it under the dog as I pulled him on top. I couldn't believe that she had us out here carrying our deceased dog. I was in so much shock that I felt like passing out. We placed him in a black garbage bag with the rest of the bags of leaves at the front of the curb. Mad as ever, I stormed back into the house to wash my hands and returned to my room. Sleep was starting to become my best friend, so I figured I'd just take a nap. It must've been one heck of a nap because I woke up just in time for dinner. "We can watch all dogs go to heaven," Grandma Mary said. Nobody laughed, but everybody ignored her and took their plate into their room. She would say some mean shit that would have you either crying your eyes out in the corner or wanting you to knock some sense into her head. I didn't even care to take my plate in the kitchen, so I sat it on my dresser and got underneath the covers.

Getting dropped off at school the next morning, I popped some gum in my mouth and went to class. Everybody was coming through the door right before the bell to rung. Today, we had to decorate our egg baby and make a bed for him or her. Another student and I passed out supplies. "My child is going to be baldheaded," Fredrick said. Everybody burst out laughing, including the teacher. We always had fun in this class, even while learning. I took strands of string and glued it to the top of the egg. With a brown marker, I put tiny dots at the cheekbone to make it look like moles. Time was up when I put on the finishing touches with a bow at the end of the bed. The student from earlier helped me put up the leftover supplies and everybody cleaned up after themselves. Today, seemed like it was going by fast as ever because next thing you know the day was out and I was getting picked up by Grandma Mary. "Where's my mom at?" I asked. "She's at the house. She's not feeling good," she said. "Why, what's wrong with her?" I questioned. "She got pneumonia," she replied. I shook my head and sat quietly in my seat. We pulled up at the house and I got out to check on my mom. I took my house key out of my pocket and went into my mom room. She looked pale, weak, and as frail as a branch on a tree with a rag covering her forehead.

Me: "Hey mom, how long are you going to be sick?"

Mom: "I don't know, but apparently I went in just in time."

Me: "Why do you say that?"

Mom: "Cause I was dehydrated and would have collapsed if I hadn't come in."

Me: "Oh ok, well you have to stay here. You can't leave us here."

Mom: "Don't even talk like that. I'll be back on my feet before you know it."

Me: "You want me to fix you something to eat or drink?"

Mom: "Yeah, bring me soup and crackers. And a cup of ice and a bottle of Sprite".

Me: "Alright, anything else you need me to do?"

Mom: "Yeah, make sure your brother and sister get their bath. And if they need some help with their homework help them or if not just check it over."

Me: "Ok, I got you."

I went into the kitchen and put pizza and cheese sticks in the oven. A feeling came over me as if someone was staring at me. Looking through the cracks of the laundry door, I saw Grandma Mary peeping through looking dead at me. Kind of creeped out I went back into my mom's room to tell her what just happened. By the time we were done talking, I heard Grandma Mary room door shut. So, I went back to the kitchen to do what I was going to do in the first place. After that, I took a shower so that I could be out of the way. Bambino was in the front room doing her homework. Larry was knocked out as soon as he came through the door, so I let him rest. Checking over Bambino's homework, I couldn't find any errors, so I told her to go take her bath. Hearing the beeping noise from the oven, I went to go pull out the pizza and cheese sticks. Larry woke up and came into the kitchen. "You're finally up," I said. He rubbed his eyes and took the plate I passed him. "After you're done go take your bath," I said. "Do you have any homework?" He shook his head no and continued eating. I sat beside him and ate.

Bambino came into the kitchen and grabbed her plate. We finished up, throwing our paper plates away and taking our drink with us into the back room. Knock! Knock! I peeped outside the window before answering. I opened the door, "Hey PaPa." "Hey, kiddo, where your ole granny at?" He asked. "She's in her room," I said. He went to go sit on the long comfy couch near the hallway closet door. Viola texted me to get on ooVoo, so I went back up the hallway to the front computer. The ring button was ringing for a little minute until she picked up at the fourth ring. We were on video chat being extra making funny faces and talking about school. Bernard said, "Who you over there talking to, Whoopi Goldberg?" I told Viola to hold on a minute and I muted myself and turned toward Bernard's direction. "I am on video chat with my friend. That was very rude of you to say," I said. He just laughed and had a stupid look on his face, as if he didn't know I would say anything about the remark he made. Like how disrespectful can you be? In the back of my mind, I couldn't get over the fact that Bernard was really starting to show his true colors. He was getting too comfortable being around us and thought that he could say or do anything he wanted without repercussions. Grandma Mary walked by and said, "Get off that video chat. That's enough chatting for today." I didn't even make a fuss because even though this was supposedly our house it seemed as if whatever Grandma Mary said it went. And I wasn't even on there long. Worse enough we can't even invite friends over. I turned around to turn the audio back on and Viola was eating Doritos. I made up an excuse as to why I had to get off and clicked out the video chat. The more Bernard started coming around the more I grew a dislike him. I went up to the hall to my room and called it a night. Smelling an aroma of some type of food and feeling the sunlight radiating heat through my window, I woke up rubbing my eyes. The house seemed quiet, so I peeked out my door to see if anybody's door was open. My mom's door was open, but I only saw my sister knocked out drooling. I walked up to the hallway into the kitchen.

Mom: "Whom the hell put some damn staples in my lima beans?"

Me: "You got to be kidding me, right?'

Mom: "I'm not playing. Look!"

Me: "I didn't do it. And Bambino and Larry is sleep so you know it can't be them. Why would somebody put lima beans in food?"

Mom: "Now I got to start off with a fresh pot. This is the shit I be talking about."

I watched as my mom scrapped the food out the pot and into the trash can. I pulled out an unopened bag of lima beans and passed it to her. Grandma Mary walked past with a plate of lima bean residue. "You put staples in these lima beans," my mom asked her. "No, wasn't none in mine," she said smirking. She opened up the refrigerator and I walked out to go to my room. I looked into the closet and saw that there was a hanger without a piece of clothing hanging on it. I grabbed it and started to place it over my head. It wouldn't fit. I heard someone pass by and threw the hanger quickly back in the closet. Slumped down in the closet, I shed silent tears hearing nothing but my breathing and heart beating fast. I was overwhelmed with going through this torture of living with Grandma Mary. I figured that if I would kill myself then the hurt I was feeling would disappear. Not only that but I was tired of seeing my mom getting mistreated by her own mother and siblings. The ones who are supposed to love and protect her were the same that mistreated her. I didn't understand how a family could be so degrading and hateful. Maybe it would be best if I was gone as it would be one person less to be worried about. Starting to feel extremely hot in the closet, I got out and hopped on my bed before anybody started looking for me. I had to pee super bad, so I did a little jog to the bathroom. After I washed my hands, I heard Grandma Mary's phone ring. So, I quickly cut the water off to see if I could hear the conversation. Slowly opening the mirror, I brought my ear closer so I could hear better. I could hear a man's voice on the other end, but I couldn't figure out who.

Grandma Mary: "Yeah, her and her kids disrespectful."

Unknown man: "What they're doing?"

Grandma Mary: "Tearing up my house, not cleaning up after themselves, and calling me out my name."

Unknown man: "Kick them out then or make it uncomfortable for them to live there."

Grandma Mary: "I need to find some type of way because I'm tired of your sister and her kids being here. They are some lucifer's."

Unknown man: "Mmmhm, they crazy."

Grandma Mary: "It sounds like I hear somebody coming. Bye."

After she said bye, I slowly closed the mirror back and was about to go into my mom's room. Grandma Mary came out of her room and smiled at me as if she wasn't just talking about us to one of her other children. I heard the game console come on in my room, so I figured that my brother was up now. But first I wanted to tell my mom what I had heard. I closed the door behind me and sat at the edge of her bed. I told her about what I had heard and we just agreed that we would stay out her way and work on getting our own place. I could tell by the look on my mom's face that she was hurt. Not just for herself but for my brother, sister, and I to have to go through being in this Devil's house with her. I walked back into my room and started playing the game with my brother and sister. My hands started getting tired, so I let the two of them play, while I read a book. It was so hot even though we had the fan on. Grandma Mary told us we weren't allowed to cut on the central air. So, we were burning up even with the chill clothes that we had on. Having the doors and windows open was no help either. I sat right in front of the fan finishing the last pages of my book. "That was a good book," I said aloud. I went into my mom's room to ask her what we were going to eat for dinner. She decided that we would order two Supreme Pizzas and a box of cinnamon sticks. We showered and got in our pajamas before the food arrived. Having a movie night, we decided to sleep in our mom's room.

Waking up the next morning, I stretched and yawned getting out of bed to go into the bathroom. Leaving out the bathroom from washing my face and brushing my teeth, I went into the kitchen, so we could start the family meeting.

Grandma Mary was standing by the sink finishing up washing her hands. Uncle Gary was standing by the barstool and Uncle Tommy was sitting at the dinner table, with my mom and I sitting across from him. Uncle Tommy's girlfriend was sitting on the couch eating chips.

Grandma: "Alright, Rochelle you can go ahead."

Mom: "So, basically mom called everyone over because we needed a little assistance here and there with the yard work. As you all know, Diana is dealing with having seizures back to back. I just came from the hospital and they said I have pneumonia and somewhat of a stomach virus. So, both of us have to take it easy until we get fully back to ourselves."

Uncle Tommy: "Well, I'm going to tell you right now. I won't be able to do it".

Me: "It's really not too much to do Uncle and I can watch the kids while you and Uncle Gary do the yard."

Uncle Tommy: "I have my own life and wife to take care of. I'm not about to come all the way over here to cut some grass."

Uncle Tommy's Gf: "Yeah, we are busy with the church and kids. We won't have time."

Mom: "Wow. But you want somebody to come over your way to babysit your kids or get you out of jail. How does that work?"

Uncle Tommy: "You all chose to do it. Nobody forcing you to."

Me: "Now come on Uncle. All we were asking for was a little help…"

Uncle Tommy: "This doesn't have anything to do with you. Stay in a child's place."

My mom got up and removed herself after her brother's rude remarks. I followed behind her to check on her because I knew her feelings were hurt and quite frankly mine were too. Some things should not be said at certain times.

The information she just found out should have been said in a private manner. Like seriously you get mad about cutting some grass and just throw it up in somebody's face that they're adopted? Hearing everybody leave the house, I told my brother and sister to stay in my room. My mom and I were discussing what just happened with the door closed. She cried for a couple of minutes in silence and later regrouped herself. Grandma Mary never came to check on her or to discuss what took place. After a while, I fixed a plate of leftovers for my mom, siblings, and I and brought it to them. Since she didn't want to feel alone, my mom decided to spend a night in my brother and I room. He helped me gather the dishes to bring them to the kitchen sink. We watched what we could find on TV until we fell asleep.

My body woke up like clockwork, from not getting much sleep. "Check your phone," my mom said. "My spirit tells me that she did something to your phone." Therefore, I called my friend's phone, but it went straight to voicemail. I called Grandma Mary phone and it did the same thing. I dialed 611 to see if they could help me figure out why my phone wasn't working. "If you have a joint owner you need to discuss with them what's going on with your account. It looks as if your phone has been placed on vacation. I am not allowed to give you any further information," the Verizon Wireless worker told me. My heart ached at that very moment. I was at a loss for words, but I didn't even know why. I should have felt that this was coming. Getting out the bed, I opened the door to knock on Grandma Mary's door to see what was going on. "Hey Grandma Mary, my phone is not working. Anything going on with your phone?"

I asked. "Nope, Bernard and I phones are working just fine," she said, slowly shutting the door in my face. Grandma Mary, Bernard, and I were on a family plan because it was cheaper, and she gave me the phone as a birthday present. And by her being the person who paid the bill I had to ask her about the situation. In my spirit, I could feel that she was lying. I could tell it all over her face and demeanor that she already knew what was going on.

While we were in the car riding to school, I started crying profusely. My grandmother looked over at me and told me I am going to be okay. She reaches over to rub my arm and I pulled away. "Do you want your phone turned back on?" She questions me. "Of course, you know I want my phone turned back on. That's the only way I can communicate back and forth with you all, friends or look up things to complete my homework and projects," I replied shaking my head. "Especially if there's an emergency. I don't even understand why my phone was even turned off in the first place." I couldn't believe that just because I stood up for her and my mom against her son, she decides to cut my phone off and give me the backlash. If anything, she should be upset with how rude and inconsiderate he was being. It's not like I'm a bad child or was being disrespectful. I didn't curse or come across as being unmanneredly towards him at all. He disrespected me, my grandma, and my mom. Getting out the car, I tried to rub my face clear of the tears that were coming down. I was walking to class and I could tell people were trying to figure out why my eyes were red. I couldn't take it anymore and broke out crying in my first block class. I cried throughout the whole time of being in that class. Students were staring at me trying to figure out why I was crying. My teacher asked me if I needed her assistance and I shook my head. The rest of the day I stayed to myself and had my head down. Friends were trying to get me to interact with them and I would just make up a lie to say why I wasn't feeling good. Indicating that it was time to go, the bell rung.

Grandma Mary picked me up in front of the school and was trying to talk to me. All the way home the car ride was silent. I didn't want to talk to her or be around her for that matter. I stepped in the house not wanting to be bothered with anything or anyone. Getting me a snack out the kitchen, I returned to my room and listened to music. My mom went in and out of my room to check on me and try to cheer me up. To clear my mind, I went to shower and put on a face mask. I then went back into my room and watched TV until it started getting dark outside. Instantly out of nowhere, I burst out crying uncontrollably. No matter how hard I tried to calm down, the tears kept flowing. I cried so much the tension in my muscles were hurting. The vein in my neck was popping out. I could feel heat escaping from my ears. A migraine started to form, and my head felt bigger than my body. Having a really rough night, I cried myself to sleep. I tossed and turned throughout the night. I was also hearing voices.

"Go kill yourself."

"Nobody loves you."

"Go do it."

"Go kill yourself."

"I hate you."

"I'm going to get you!"

"I'm going to kill you."

These demonic voices were clouding my mind. I grabbed my bible to read a few pages, let it lay in the bed with me, and prayed myself to sleep. Rolling over in the bed, I got up stretching, hearing my bones pop. I looked over in the bed to see my brother sleep. Knocking on my mom's door, I waited for her to open the door.

Mom: "Good Morning Pooh, you want to help me cook some breakfast?"

Me: "Yeah, let me use the bathroom first."

Mom: "Before you use it, turn the knob on the toilet because she keeps turning it off."

Me: "Why? Is something wrong with the toilet?"

Mom: "Nope. I think she just picking. So, just be sure to turn it off after you use the toilet and don't flush."

Me: "Oh ok…."

Me: "Last night I had a hard time sleeping. It's like the devil was attacking me. It wanted me to kill myself, but once I started praying it went away."

Mom: "It's okay Pooh. Keep praying. We are going to get through this. Never forget God is always in control. Now go ahead and use the restroom so you can help me cook."

I was really starting to believe this house was like hell. The only thing we were allowed to do was breathe. Going into the bathroom, I peed and check to make sure the knob was turned off as my mom told me. I washed my hands and told my mom that I was ready. She closed her door and followed me to the kitchen. I pulled a bowl out of the cabinet and a big spoon from the drawer. In the bowl, I poured some pancake mix and a bit of water. I made a total of eight pancakes and my mom cooked the eggs and sausages. We made our plate and went into the front room to watch TV. The shows that we once had were now back on. Taking advantage of the timing, we caught up on old shows we used to watch. Larry woke up and went into the kitchen to fix his plate. He sat on the floor watching TV with us. "Diana, you want to play the game?" he pleaded. We played the Nemo game on the GameCube for an hour or so. Then, we started getting tired and just wanted to watch TV. He took the cords out and switched it to TV mode. Flipping through the channels, the majority of them were blacked out. We looked at each other in confusion as to why this was happening. We went into our mom's room to see if her TV looked the same way because my mom and I were just watching TV and it was perfectly fine. She cut on the TV to see if it was the same as ours.

Mom: "She must've cut off certain channels."

Brother: "But mom, why?"

Me: "Well it looks like she cut off the ones that are our favorite."

Brother: "Does that mean we can't watch what we use to watch anymore?"

Mom: "Just watch what you all can watch. Or get you all's DVD player and watch some movies on it. It's going to be okay."

My brother and I went back into our room. He set up the DVD player and picked a movie from the box of DVDs and tapes he had. He ended up picking Shrek 2, while I got us some popcorn from the kitchen. I started feeling sleepy, so I made sure Larry didn't have to use the bathroom. I pulled some boxes and bags out of our closet in front of our door. I found a toy that made noise when bumped and placed it on top of one of the boxes. I wanted to make sure that I could hear if somebody was trying to open the door. We caught Grandma Mary in our room a couple of times and her excuse was always "she was praying over us". Just when I was about to fall asleep, I heard the doorknob turn, so I eased up in my bed. Grandma Mary had her head peeked into the crack of the door saying, "Oh, I was just checking on you all". Going back out the door, she went back into her room. I tiptoed up to the door and pushed the stuff back up against the door again and went back to bed.

The next day was Teacher's Work Day. Unfortunately, at this moment I would have rather been at school than at home. I got up and removed the bags and boxes from the door. It was really boring without having my phone. Well, having a phone without any service, but to only play games. I went into my mom's room to see if we were doing anything for the day. She told me to go wash my face and brush my teeth, so when the other two woke up we could run to the store. To pass time, I helped her fold the laundry while we watched TV. Minutes passed by and everybody was ready to go. We hopped in the truck and went to Walmart. Picking up some groceries for the house, we filled up the basket to compacity. After spending about twenty minutes at the checkout, we loaded the car and headed home. Pulling up to the house, everybody helped bring in the groceries. While they were bringing the groceries in something told me to hide some of the items. So, making sure not to get caught I looked around to make sure nobody was around me. I hid towels, rags, drinks, chips, soap, toilet tissue, and anything else my spirit led me to hide in my closet. Playing it off, I went into the kitchen to finish helping put the groceries in their rightful place. My mom cooked salmon, asparagus, and mash potatoes for dinner. We ate in the front room while watching whatever we could find on TV. My siblings finished their food and decided to go in the room to play Mortal Kombat. Grandma Mary came through asking why we're not spending time with her. I continue to stare into the TV.

Grandma Mary: "Come on let's have a family meeting."

Me: "I'm tired of having these meetings. Nothing is done to fix the problems."

Mom: "Let's just listen to what she has to say."

Grandma Mary: "So what seems to be the problem."

Me: "There's a lot of problems. Let me start off by asking why my phone got turned off? Everybody at school is asking me what's wrong with my phone and I'm lying and trying to make up excuses as to what could be going on."

Grandma Mary: "Don't worry about your phone. I called the people and they said it'll come back on."

Me: "So why did it get turned off in the first place?"

Mom: "You know she's going to lie anyway…"

Grandma Mary: "They said something happened to the towers."

Me: "Yeah ok."

Mom: "Why is it that your children keep attacking me and Diana?"

Grandma Mary: "I don't know why they're messing with you all. I keep telling them to leave you alone."

Me: "And how come they "supposedly" know what we have going on over here and we don't have a phone. I don't have a phone and mama phone hasn't come in the mail yet. So, evidently, that means you're telling them lies of what we're doing over here."

Grandma Mary: "I haven't told them anything."

Mom and Me: "Yeah, ok."

Me: "Grandma Mary sometimes I feel like I don't even know you anymore."

Grandma Mary: "And I feel like I don't know you anymore either."

Silence fell upon us, and we stared each other down for a good ten to twenty minutes. Not once did she blink. Irritated and taken back by her comment, I looked at my mom and told her I was done with this conversation. It gets really old when someone tries to play the victim or act like they don't have a clue as to what's going on. I truly loved my family but with everything that was going on, we were getting torn farther apart. People's egos, jealousy, and misinformation were getting in the way of having a relationship with each other. The drama was spreading like wildfires and I couldn't find a hose big enough to put it out. I decided to go to sleep in my mom's room. Before getting in the bed, I helped my mom push her dresser in front of the door. She turned on her TV to the gospel station, we prayed and went to sleep.

"Rise and shine," my mom said knocking on the dresser. Pulling the covers off me, I got up to go in the bathroom. I sat on the toilet for a few minutes to regroup my thoughts. Then, I brushed my teeth and washed my face. I was too tired to stand up, so I took a bath and then wrapped up in a towel to go put my clothes on in the room. Larry was in the bathroom getting dressed, while Bambino was in mom's room getting dressed. We grabbed us a banana before heading out the door. Going up to my school, I got out of the truck and waved back. The truck went off into the distance with the music bumping loud. "Diana, come here," somebody yelled. I looked around to see what direction the voice was coming from. My homeboy Christopher was at the table sitting down twirling a string from his bookbag in his hands. We talked about random stuff and talked some more when friends came around. I got up and walked to class, hearing the bell go off. The class was going well since today was our Spring Fling we really weren't doing much. We were in homeroom with everybody doing their own thing. Some were having small talk, some sleeping, and others were playing board games. A few hours later the bell rang and we were allowed to go outside to the event.

I met up with my friends and walked around to find what we wanted to eat. We saw a food truck with wings on it and decided to go there. Ordering some buffalo wings and a side of bacon cheese fries, I stepped to the side to let the rest of my friends order their food. We ate some pizza and played some games. There was a group of people surrounding the mic, as a tall boy was freestyling, and everybody was cheering him on. After hours of walking around and having fun, we wrapped up and headed to our ways of transportation. Today, I was riding the bus, so I got on and pulled down the window. The bus driver pulled up at my destination and I walked down to my house. Walking into the driveway, I saw the red truck wasn't parked. So, I figured my mom was running an errand. I opened the door and I heard sobbing.

Me: "Why are you crying? What's wrong? What happened?"

Mom: "Bernard. He took…He took…"

Me: "He took the truck, didn't he?"

Mom: "Yeah, he took the truck. Talking about he told me that he wanted $1,200 for it."

Me: "I thought Grandma Mary said just to get insurance on it and then, it's yours."

Me: "What about the payments you were already giving him? If it's like that then he needs to give you your money back because Grandma Mary didn't say that."

Mom: "That's what I'm saying. Evidently, she must've lied. Now I got to look for another car all over again."

Mom: "It seems like when I take ten steps forward, I get pushed back twenty. I just can't win for losing."

Me: "Who picking Bambino and Larry up?"

Mom: "They are riding the bus home."

Mom: "But that's not it either. He threw the stuff I had in the truck out on the ground."

Me: "What???"

Me: "Okay, don't worry about it, mom. We will find another car. I'm going to help you. And as for him, you know what I will just keep my mouth closed."

Mom: "Look, I think that's her car that just passed by."

We went outside and hid behind the bush. Looking up the street, we spotted Grandma Mary's car posted at the corner of the block. It was so weird seeing her just sit at the end of the corner as if she's scoping out a crime scene. We went back inside when we saw her car inch forward. I looked down at my watch to see what time it was. Ten minutes later Bambino and my brother Larry arrived. I helped Bambino with her homework while mom helped Larry with his. After that, the kids went to go take their shower and get into their pajamas. I went on the computer in the front room to look up some used car places and wrote down their numbers, while my mom cooked us dinner. Afterward, I gave her the list and went to take my shower. Putting on my pajamas, I walked towards the kitchen to get a plate of food. My mom called around to different car lots and the outcome looked slim to none. Getting frustrated, she decided to take her shower. I went into the kitchen to make her a plate of food, so when she came out of the bathroom she could eat. I was exhausted and irritated myself. If it wasn't one thing it was another. To comfort my mom, I decided to sleep in her room for the night. "There got to be better days," I thought to myself. In the darkness of her room, silence fell upon us as I cried and prayed myself to sleep.

Hearing the bird chirps woke me from my sleep. I peeped through my blinds wishing I could see Beast at my window jumping up trying to see if I was in my room. Suddenly, I remembered that I had a book meeting and needed to get ready. I quickly showered and put my clothes on. I was in the middle of asking my mom if she could take me when Grandma Mary offered to since she had an errand to run. We pulled up at the library and I opened the car door and went inside. Waving to the librarian, I greeted her with a smile. I walked all the way into the back to the conference room and took my seat to wait for the others to arrive. We discussed our book of the month for about an hour and a half. Wrapping up, we said our final thoughts and goodbyes. Coming out of the library, I saw my mom, brother, and sister walking towards me. "Check your phone. She was in the car talking about us, lying, and looking at us crazy," my mom told me. I looked down at my phone turning up the brightness. Texts and voicemails started flooding my phone to the point it was saying low memory.

Auntie Vicky: "What you doing to my mama?"

Uncle Gary: "Stop disrespecting your grandma and go tell her you're sorry."

Auntie Vicky: "Keep disrespecting my mama and I will call Juvenile on you. Stop beating on her car window."

Uncle Tommy: "You need to learn to stay in a child's place."

Uncle Gary: "You, your siblings, and your mom have been disrespecting her long enough. It's time that you all to get up out of her house."

Uncle Gary: "Respect is key in everything that you do. We all love you and want the best for you. But the disrespect coming from you all need to go."

Me: "Wow. I can't believe this. Look at all these texts."

Mom: "They're blowing my phone up too."

Me: "Don't worry about it. Let's just get back in the car and ignore her."

Revving up the engine, she speeds up the car driving erratic on the main street, swerving in and out of lanes. We were yelling for her to slow down since the normal talking to her wasn't getting through to her. "Stop the car and pull over," my mom said. "Where you all are going?" My grandma asked. At first, she wouldn't stop but after a while I guess she changed her mind. My mom, sister, brother, and I got out of the car and walked to the house. Grandma Mary disappeared down the road to wherever she was going. We finally made it to the house full of anger and hurt. It was crazy to think that the very people (family) that are closest to you would stab you in the back.

Mom: "We have to get up out of here. She trying to get me sent to jail and call CPS, so she can take me away from you all."

Me: "We definitely need to get out of here. She trying to get me locked up, too. It would be a cold day in hell because we're not going with CPS or her. I'm telling you that right now."

Siblings: "We're not going with anybody."

Mom: "Get back from the curb. Hide behind that bush. She's sitting at the edge of the street looking down this way."

Me: "That's weird. She's just sitting there watching us."

Mom: "It's something gotten into her."

Siblings: "Why is she acting like this, mom?"

Mom: "I don't know. I guess that's what happens when you tell lies and you have to remember what lie you told to cover that lie."

Me: "What are we going to do in the meantime, though?"

Mom: "Let's go in the house and start boxing up our stuff. I'm about to call Ryan."

My mama called her guy friend Ryan and told him to come to the house. He showed up and instantly started helping us bring out our belongings to his truck. We pulled into the Super 8 Hotel up the street. Everybody gathered up the items and brought them into the hotel room and pacing their steps feeling uncomfortable as to where things may lead next. Making this big move, I knew I had to step up and keep my mom and siblings protected by any means necessary. Breaking the silence, Tim asked, "So how long you all plan to stay here? Are you all going to go back?" I spoke up, "We don't want to ever go back." "Hold on, let me talk to you all mom for a minute," he said turning towards the door. He and my mom went outside the door, I'm guessing to talk about how things were going to go. He left to go get us food and then, left to go to his Dad's house. His dad was very sick at the time dealing with health issues. My mom, brother, sister, and I all showered and divided into two beds. While my brother and sister were sleep, my mom and I stayed up to discuss what we were going to do. We even went as far as thinking about shelters to stay and man, that was the last place I wanted to end up! Seeing my mother break down was like seeing shattered glass on the floor broken into millions of pieces and not knowing how to clean up the mess. I got her to calm down, reassured her that we were going to be okay, and prayed myself to sleep.

Guess what day it was the next morning? Thanksgiving! A day, where we should be surrounded by family and loved ones, enjoying the food that my mom MOSTLY cooked, which was a daily task for her every day anyway. Instead, it had become a day that turned into a battlefield of depressing emotions. We had no one to turn to or no one to call. We reached out to so many people including all family members and no one helped! We called a police officer in the family that we knew of and the only thing the person said for us to do was to call a shelter. That's what you say to family, right? Like who really wants to live in a shelter! Nobody could give us a room to share or a floor to sleep on, which we would have been fine with until we were able to get back on our feet. Throughout the day, we received texts from family members saying Happy Thanksgiving, while others were sending threats telling us to go back or to stay in the streets. They didn't take out the time to see what was going on. I felt like they didn't even care at all. I felt disgusted and disrespected as to their demeanor toward us. My mama got in touch with Menistroso, our cousin, to see when we could move in. When Menistroso found out that we were in need of a place to stay she offered that we could stay with her and her family.

"Menistroso's mother is coming over to bring us some food," my mother said after she hung up the phone. We stayed at the hotel for about three days or so. That was until our cousin, Menistroso, pulled up into the parking lot to help us get our stuff out the hotel and take it to her house. We were nervous and hesitant, but we didn't have anywhere else to go. No place to call home and no transportation to get around. We took a leap of faith and went along. Upon arriving, looking at the small bricked house, we got out and made our way into the house to settle in. Their daughter, Theresa, gave up her room so that my mother and sister could sleep in there. While my brother and I slept in the room with the other two boys. Going into where my mother and sister were at, our boxes covered Theresa's room. I showed my mom the items that I had hid when we were back at Grandma Mary's house. She was puzzled as to how I had tissue, pads, drinks, etc. "You all can go play," Menistroso said. "Take them outside." I asked my mom was she okay with us going outside. We followed her kids outside the backdoor. Stepping into the backyard, I saw tons of leaves covering the grass. We went outside and played on the trampoline. Getting tired of that, I saw a ball near one of the cars, picked it up, and began dribbling it between my legs. I ran towards the goal and made a layup. Everybody started coming over by me to shoot the ball. We stayed outside for a while until it was time to come in for dinner. I didn't like how they cooked a separate meal from the kids, but our mom gave us some food off her plate, and we ate what Menistroso and her husband cooked for the kids, as well. It was time to get ready for bed. So, my brother gathered his pajamas and went into the bathroom first. Next, my mother and sister went, while I watched our belongings. Last but not least, I went into the bathroom showered and quickly dressed. It felt so strange being at someone else's house. I also wondered if they were peeping in the bathroom while I showered, so I would quickly be in and out. Besides, I didn't want them to go off on us about running up the water bill or taking too long. We stayed up talking about our situation and how we couldn't believe we were in this predicament. It was truly unbelievable to be forced out of a house that we shared with a family member that we thought would never turn on us. It was truly like living in hell there. Getting out of my head, I finally went to sleep.

Tossing and turning in the middle of the night, I lifted up my head seeing the room full of boxes, remembering where I was at. I couldn't sleep so I stared at the ceiling until everybody got up. Eventually, my mom woke up a little after me. We talked about making a way out, coping with our emotions, and getting back on our feet. Menistroso was up cooking eggs, sausages, grits, and toast. After she was done, we fixed a plate to eat. Menistroso asked my mom if she needed to go anywhere. So, my mom showered and got dressed to go with her to pick up some groceries and to the library. I stayed at the house to watch the kids and prepare for school the next day. By the time they were long gone up the street, my siblings and the other kids were waking up. I told them where they were going and they went into the kitchen to get something to eat. The middle child poured himself a big bowl of Chocolate Frosted Flakes, while everybody else got some of the breakfast Menistroso cooked. I made sure that my brother and sister cleaned up behind themselves after they were done eating. Taking their mind off what was going on around them, I went into the room and played hangman and Uno with them. I made sure we were showered and into our pajamas, so it could take some stress off our mom. Packing their bookbag, I heard a knock at the door. I peep through the peephole to see who it is. Opening the door, I see my mom and Menistroso with bags in their hand. I helped them bring the groceries into the house and put them away. After my mom was settled, she thanked me for helping her out and always being her backbone. She told me that she put in countless job applications. And, I told her to go relax and to take her shower. My mom cooked dinner this time and I was so glad because I really missed her cooking. Everybody's plates were cleaned spotless and bellies were full. Everybody went off to bed.

Dropping me off at the bus stop the next morning was very interesting. Looking through the window, I spotted my grandmother in the corner of the bus stop gazing at the bus. Then, she spotted me and just stared. It was so weird and uncomfortable due to not living with her anymore, but she popped up at the bus stop only to stare me down. I didn't understand why she was scoping out my environment as if she cared in the first place. I texted my mom to tell her that I saw Grandma Mary at the bus stop and told them to be careful. I was mad that I had to ride the bus to school because I didn't feel comfortable leaving my brother and sister behind, in the hands of people I barely knew, even though they seemed like fairly decent people. The bus driver pulled up to the school and we fell in line off the bus. I walked over to the table where my friends and I always met up. We chatted about Mr. Andy's class and how we could barely understand what he said. The bell rang and everybody scattered to wherever they were going. I was glad the first block was over with it because it was the same girl who was loud first thing in the morning every day. Like damn, she doesn't ever shut up. Next class was drama, one of my favorite classes. I loved acting and pretending to be a whole other person. Finishing up my monologue, I sat down in my seat as everybody was still clapping. The last ten minutes of class we chatted with friends until it was time to go. With my heavy backpack on my back, I moved along the traffic of the hall to my next class. Along the way, I stopped to talk to some friends. At last, it was time to pack up for dismissal. I did my usual routine of taking the back way to get to the bus and climbed aboard. Waiting on the last few to get on, the bus driver turned the key to start the engine.

We made it to our stop and shuffled out the doors. A car passed by, not caring that we were getting off the bus. I got into the car and put my seat belt on. This time I was the only one in the car because everybody else was already at home or made it early off the bus. Putting my bookbag down in the corner of the room, I walked back out to pour a glass of apple juice. Returning back to the room, I started a conversation with my mom.

Me: "Hey mom, what are you doing?"

Mom: "About to fold up these clothes. How was your day?"

Me: "It was good. I did my monologue today and everybody really liked it. My teacher told me I should sign up for Drama 2."

Mom: "Oh ok, that's good. You know you can do whatever you put your mind to, but make sure all your important classes are out of the way first."

Me: "Yeah, I know. Any luck with the jobs?"

Mom: "Dollar Tree called me and told me I got the job. So, I had to go up there and fill out some paperwork."

Me: "Well that's what's up. It's a start to something."

Mom: "Yeah, it is. I just want to get you all up out of here, so you all can have your own space and privacy."

Me: "Yeah, I know mom. But you are doing good. Don't beat yourself up. You, sticking by our side is the main thing right now. We got this."

Mom: "Yeah, and I meant to tell you too. I switched our mail over and made sure to take your grandma off you and your siblings' paperwork at school. So, if she tries to pick you up from school, tell them no and to call the police."

Me: "Okay, I got you. Is dinner cooked?"

Mom: "Yeah, she cooked not too long ago."

Me: "Alright, I'm about to fix me and the kids a plate. You want me to fix yours?"

Mom: "No, just do you all. Thanks."

Me: "Ok, I love you, mom."

Mom: "I love you too, Pooh."

I fixed my siblings and I plate. Mostly macaroni filled my plate. Biting into the ribs, I smacked my lips. The barbecue sauce was smacking. Finishing up, I went to go wash my hands and lay down. "Grandma Mary chained my hands and feet up to a chair. I had duct tape covering my mouth. Even with the opening of my nose, it felt like I was gasping for air. There wasn't a window in sight, which made the room feel extra dark. She left the room and told me that she would be back. Men and women in all black came out of nowhere and started yelling in my face. I didn't even feel the tears rolling down my face as I rocked in the chair trembling from fear." Waking up in a cold sweat, I looked around to see that it was only a nightmare that I was having. My heart was beating fast and I thought it was going to jump out of my chest. I inhaled and exhaled slowly to calm my breathing.

Christmas break arrived and everyone was excited to not have school or homework. My mom was glad to be home with us, but she was also irritated because it was hard finding a job. Dollar Tree was not giving her enough days or hours. She wanted us to have a place of our own, a stable job, and not worry about having to depend on anyone for anything. Going to Dollar Tree was becoming a waste of time and gas, so she had to quit. We had Christmas music playing, while the kids were decorating the tree. "Who wants to put the star up?" Menistoso asked. "I want to do it," Theresa said. She stepped on the ladder, while her dad held onto it so she wouldn't fall. I wasn't really in the mood for Christmas. All I could think about was my mom, brother, sister, and I at someone else's home not having anywhere to go and feeling abandoned. I was thankful to have a roof over my head but was also ready for us to have a place of our own. Menistroso pulled out some gingerbread houses and we started pulling out the supplies to build them. I could tell my mom was tired, but I could also tell that she wasn't giving up without a fight. Before we went to bed, we set cookies out for "Santa". My brother, sister, and I didn't believe in Santa. We learned pretty early that our mom or grandmother was the one buying presents.

The next day arrived and the front room light was on. Menistroso's children were unwrapping the gifts they received. My brother, sister, and I unwrapped our gifts. We were actually shocked that we were receiving anything because we understood it was a tough time for our mom. But luckily two of her siblings were able to send us some items. We were thankful to have something, and we took it with a smile. We cleaned up the wrapping paper and went to go try out our new toys and watch TV. In the room, I walked in on my mom crying. "What's wrong?" I asked. "I feel like I let you all down. I should've left her house a long time ago. We wouldn't even be in this predicament." "Mom, it's going to be okay. We got to stay strong. Remember, winning is our protocol." I said trying to cheer her up. "God is in control." Later that night, I prayed a long prayer and watched until the last person closed their eyes to sleep.

The next day, I arrived at the bus stop, being that I was the first one to always get dropped off because my school was the farthest away from the house. Stepping onto the bus, I found my seat and put my headphones in. I liked peace in the morning and couldn't stand loud noises or people being loud in the morning time. Sitting down at the table, I waited patiently for my friends to show up. The bell rung, so it was time for us to go to our first block. I hated having Algebra first thing in the morning. I loved math, but when they started adding letters and punctuation marks, it started getting complicated. The teacher didn't make it any easier because she wanted us to show our work exactly how she did in class. But the only problem I had with that was we're not always going to get math problems exactly how she taught us. There are multiple ways to solve math problems. Leaving that class, I went to the restroom. "What's up, Diana? Get to class before I whoop you," my homeboy said. Pushing through the door, I went into a stall and urinated. I washed my hands and came out. The rest of the day seemed to be going smooth. Teachers and students were cracking jokes while we did our work. The bell rung for lunch and everybody scattered to the next location. I didn't like school lunch, so I would bring my own. Walking outside, I saw friends already at our table. Buzz! Buzz! My phone was ringing and vibrating non-stop.

Me: "Hello, mom, are you okay?"

Mom: "Girl no, she got me up here in the car riding around with her, while she is selling stuff out her house."

Me: "What in the world, that's dangerous. What's the stuff she's selling?"

Mom: "Belts and shoes..."

Mom: "And I think she's doing prostitution and suggesting that I do it."

Me: "What the…Why you say that?"

Mom: "In the driver side, she got a belt and cologne. On the side of my seat, there is a box of condoms and Listerine. Then, she made a joke about saran wrap."

Me: "You better be careful. You need me to do anything."

Mom: "No, just keep your phone close. I wanted you to know my whereabouts. We not too far from the house. So, if anything goes down. I'm walking my ass to the house."

Me: "Okay, love you. Talk to you later."

Mom: "Love you too."

Hanging up the phone, I try to play it smooth like nothing was going on. I talked to my friends before it was time to go to our last class of the day. Nobody knew what was going on at school. None of the students or staff. I felt like if I told I would end up in Foster Care making matters worse, so I would try my best to act okay at school. Art class was fun and also nerve-wracking at times because some of the students didn't want to cooperate during the lecture. Finally, it was time to go home. I walked to the bus and sat in my seat. The bus driver was very picky and didn't like for us to eat on the bus. I would sneak and eat or drink anyway. I was not about to pass out from hunger or thirst. Stopping at the bus stop, she waited for us to get off. I opened the car door and slid in. "Hey you all! How was your day? Where's my mom?" I asked. "It was busy but good. And she's at the house doing her hair. How was your day?" Menistrorso replied. "It was good. Thanks for asking," I smiled slightly, sitting back in my seat. We picked up the rest of the kids and headed back to the house. Everybody went in their own direction to go do their homework or get a snack. I walked into the back room to see what my mom was doing.

Mama: "Hey Diana, how was your day?"

Me: "Hey mom, it was straight. What about yours besides what you already told me?"

Mama: "Where your brother and sister at?"

Me: "They in the living room doing their homework."

Mama: "Ok, good. Close the door, so I can tell you the rest of what happened."

Me: "Alright. Let me put my bookbag down."

Mama: "So, tell me why when we got back to the house there was an eviction notice on the door?"

Me: "Oh wow, and when were they going to tell us. If they're getting evicted, where in the world we are going?"

Mama: "That's what I'm saying. We got to find a way up out of here. God needs to come on because we're drowning."

Me: "He really does. All we can do is keep holding onto faith. He will see us through. We can't give up."

Mama: "Yeah I know. It's just so hard."

I pulled out my homework and completed it within minutes. It was very boring, so I went to take a shower and went to sleep. The following morning, I woke up to my mom and sister watching TV. Walking into the bathroom, I closed the door so I could pee and do my hygiene. I walked into the room to grab my house shoes and my mom phone started ringing. Looking at it, I didn't recognize the number.

Me: "Mama, your phone is ringing."

Mama: "Who is it? Answer it."

Me: "Hello, may I ask who's calling?"

Unknown Person: "Hi, this is Andrew at Morrisons. Giving you a call to tell you that you got the job and you can start tomorrow if you would like."

Mama: "Okay, great. What time should I be there?"

Andrew: "Be here at 8."

Mama: "Okay, thank you. See you there."

Andrew: "You're welcome. Have a great day."

My mama and I were jumping up and down after hearing the good news. This was definitely a start for us getting our own car and place. My siblings came into the room hearing us clapping. We told them the good news and they were just as excited as we were. We were hugging, smiling, and all laughing. God was really working things out in our favor. We just had to be patient and continue to fight hard, instead of drowning in sorrow. Menistroso and her family were gone away from the house for a little while. So, we were at the house working out a plan to get us where we wanted to be. I even started putting in applications to see if someone would hire me, but everyone was saying I wasn't old enough yet. Asking a boy at school if I could sell some pills for him is how far I went to make some money. "You're too smart for that. I'm not giving you these pills," he said. I really think he thought I was just talking, but I was serious. I wanted up out of that house and into our own. Anyway, I got the hair supplies so my mom could do my hair. It took her about two hours to finish and she started doing my sister's hair. My brother and I showered and got our bookbag ready for school. By that time, Menistroso and her family came back and got settled into the house. I put my phone on the charger and got ready for bed. Soon as I got into a deep sleep, I felt a hand rub on my butt. Opening my eyes, I see Stanley's hand on me and he quickly took it off. "Oh, I'm sorry. I didn't mean to," he said. I leaned up as I was processing what just happened and what to do next. If I tell will they kick us out? Not worrying about what will happen next, I woke my mama up and told her what happened. She said, "What you want to do? You want to call the police or tell his parents?" I went to go tell his parents and they started cursing him out. "You know that's your mother fucking cousin right," Menistoroso yelled. "No. I didn't even try to touch her though. My hand slipped," he lied.

Ch5 Back to Hell or Off to Heaven

We couldn't take living in our house anymore. So, we made the best decision we could. Actually, we really didn't have a choice. I mean we could have gone to a shelter, but nobody wants to go there. Our family turned their back on us. We could run no longer; therefore, we called my grandmother Mary and asked if we could come back. She came to where we were at and helped pack our belongings into her red truck. It was strange being back in a familiar place that we once called home. As we settled in, I watched TV in the living room. Mary came over and sat next to me, placed her hand on the top of my knee and said, "I heard what you went through and I want to know that if you ever need to talk, I'm here for you." Unconsciously, I looked down at my knee and couldn't do anything but nod my head. In my head, I thought why in the hell would I tell you anything when you were a snake in wools clothing? She got up from the couch and went into the kitchen. I cut the TV off and went into the room I used to stay in, locked the door, and went to sleep.

The next day everybody went off to school and work. Towards the end of the day, while I was at school, I received a text from my mother saying that she was picking me up from school. I was happy because I didn't feel like riding the bus. I wanted to go home and get something to eat. Ding! Ding! Ding! The dismissal bell rang, and I met up at the spot I told my mother to pick me up from. I hurried to the car, got in, and put on my seatbelt. "Whose car is this?" I asked. "Ours! Got it off the lot, today and I just need to get the tags," she replied.

I turned the radio on and turned the volume to the max. Blasting music was our way of celebrating and rejoicing for God bringing us out of the storm. We went to go pick up my siblings from school and they were ecstatic to see the new car. We knew we were very close to leaving my grandmother's house for good. Pulling up into the driveway, we sat and talked about how our day went and where things were heading.

Luckily, Grandma Mary wasn't at the house, so my brother and sister went to take their bath, while my mother and I went to cook dinner. I pulled out the spices we needed, while she pulled out the ingredients. Setting the temperature, I placed the ribs in the oven. My mother wiped down the counter and walked to the back. Hearing the front door open, I followed right behind her. The kids had their pajamas on and were watching TV. I showered, put on my clothes, and went into the kitchen to fix my siblings and I plate. My grandmother fixed her plate and went to her room. My mom fixed her plate and sat by my brother. We finished off the day by watching Caroline. The next day my mother had gone off to work and I went to go see if my grandmother could take me to a few places. "Hey, I want to go looking for jobs today, but my mom had to go in early, can you take me?" I ask her. "Oh yeah, sure," she replied. My siblings and I were already dressed, so we waited in the living room for her to get ready. I turned off the TV and walked to the door as she came up the hallway.

We rode around Faust street, stopping at fast-food and retail spots. We pulled up to Burger King and I went in to speak to the manager. I left with a good feeling and decided to call it a day. I came back to the car and told my grandmother that we could go back to the house. We pulled up to the house and everybody went to their room. A couple of hours later my mom entered the house and came into our rooms to see if we ate. I told her that I made them leftovers and made sure they took a bath before she came home. She took her a bath, ate, and climbed in the bed with us. We talked for a little bit and then my mother led us in prayer. I got up to make sure the door was locked, and I took a box from the closet and sat it close to the door. I slid back in the bed and drifted off to sleep.

Three days later, I received a call from Burger King and they told me what I needed to do to get the job and which day they were available for an interview. I went to get my food-handlers card, did the interview, and was hired!

Eleventh grade was going well and my birthday was around the corner. Everybody was dressed and ready to get the day started. I knew we were going over my best-friend, Tami, house to pick her up, but that's all I knew. We pulled up at her house and we entered her front room. She had giftbags laid out on the table for me. I went through them and it seems she knew exactly what to get me. She got me a hat that I was eyeing at Spencer's, lotion from Victoria Secret, and a matching necklace. I hugged her and she grabbed her purse to ride with us. On our way to our next destination, my mother got a call. Looking at her facial expression, I could tell she was beaming with happiness. "So, NaNa, I just got the news that the apartment is approved and ready, and we can move in today. It's up to you, if you want to go have fun or move in today", she said looking at me. "Skip that let's move in," I said turning the music up.

We rode over to the house and walked through the door. My mother knocked on my grandmother's door and told her that we were moving. Everybody went to their rooms and started boxing up their clothes, shoes, and other important items. My mother started packing up the items in the bathroom; however, my grandmother tried to intervene in what she was taking, saying that it was hers, but my mom continued to pack, ignoring what my grandmother was saying. We loaded the car and went to Sunshine Apartments. My grandmother loaded her car and brought over some stuff. My mom made a couple more trips back and forth, leaving nothing but our beds and dressers. Before it got too late, we dropped Tami back off at her house. Pulling up to Taco Bell, we ordered tacos and cinnamon delights. When we got back to the house, we ate, my mother got a notebook and wrote down a list of items we needed. Then, she drew out how she wanted the kitchen, living, and dining room to be. I pulled out the electric blow up mattress we used when we were homeless and turned it on. Everybody took their baths and came back downstairs to go to sleep.

A couple of months later, we all got baptized except for my sister. She didn't go through with it because she feared drowning. Life was going well and we were making great progress within the apartment. There wasn't a peep from family members going off on us anymore or us wondering where we were going to lay our head. Happiness was moving itself back in. One day while we were unpacking some of our boxes and cleaning upstairs, my mother told me to come here and listen to a song. After, I put some clothes into the closet, we met each other almost halfway and I put my ear to her phone. I started crying, covering my mouth. Just thinking back on all the obstacles I went through just to see me now loving myself and thanking God for carrying me was a tremendous breakthrough. My mom hugged me and said, "Baby everything is going to be all right. We are free now with a place of our own." These were not just tears of pain that I let out, but also tears of joy in finding out who I really am and understanding my purpose.

When I was looking for guidance, God sent me a mentor, Mrs. Watkins. She was a very friendly lady, who encouraged me to get to know myself more and step out of conforming to what society believed to be correct. I was really getting on a good path of learning myself all over again. Although I was already mature, it seemed as if my matureness was too much for some people to handle. Tami and I got into a big argument and are no longer friends. I tried to reconcile and put our differences to the side, but whatever I did just didn't seem to be enough. I was used to riding solo and being my own best friend, but of course, it hurt to see our friendship end. But I knew for sure that I was a great friend and would be there for her if she ever needed anything, even after she turned her back on me.

Ch6 How "Green" Are You?

Waking up one early morning, I went to the bathroom to take a shower. I got out and wrapped up in my towel. Before I went to my room, I knocked on my mom's and brother's door to see if they were up. Going into my room, I put lotion on and got ready for school. The door pushes open and my sister entered to retrieve her shoes. I grabbed my wallet, bookbag, and phone and headed downstairs. Realizing I left my gum, I turned around and picked it up off my dresser. Everybody was dressed and ready to go. My mother dropped my brother and sister off first and then headed off towards Halls Mills Rd. to drop me off. We pulled over on the side of the road behind the car that was slowing in front of us. "You got everything? Have a good day at school," she said. "Yeah, alright. Love you." I replied. She said, "I love you too" and I closed the door, watching her go off in a distance. Walking over to the portables, I saw Alexis coming towards my direction. "Aye, my home-boy said he wants to talk to you," Alexis said. "What homeboy? Do I know him?" I ask her. "You'll see," she said. As I turned around, I saw a tall dark-skinned guy smiling and waving his hand. "Hey Diana, would you like to be my girlfriend? I should've been asked you, but I um…" "Sure," I said. And just like that, I became the girlfriend of a boy I didn't know much about.

I mean I knew a little about him because we attended the same middle school, but that was about it. I was so "green" about relationships. I didn't know what questions to ask, how to act, or what to say. But I was like why not, what do I have to lose? From that day forward, we talked heavily and the vibe was alright. But something was off and something about our relationship just didn't feel right. Being hardheaded, I didn't listen to my intuition and break up with him. Instead, I just went ahead with the ride. I would meet him in his first block class in the morning since we were close by. One day I came in and he tried to dismiss me. Just walked out and left, so I decided to leave him a note before I left, thinking he was just having a bad morning. Later that evening, he called me.

"Hey Sweets, how are you doing," he asked?"

"I'm doing good. Today, school was a breeze and I didn't have to work, so that's a plus."

"Awe, that's good. And my day was alright. Just ready to graduate you know?"

"Yeah, I hear you, but know that you can always talk to me about anything."

"Thanks, but I don't really like to bother people with my issues."

"You're not a bother at all. That's part of being in a relationship. You should feel comfortable about coming to me for anything even if it's about me."

"Well, I guess you're right. Oh yes, I meant to ask if you are available this coming Saturday. It's my mom's birthday and we're going out to eat."

"Yeah, I'm clear on my end, but let me make sure that my mom is cool with it. Hold on."

I went to ask my mom if she had anything to do and if I could go. Getting her approval, I relayed the news and we got off the phone. I went to shower and get a snack from the kitchen. Going back to my room, I cut on the TV to watch Netflix until I fell asleep. I was snoring until I heard a knock on my door and I slightly opened my eyes to see my mother standing in front of me holding a lump sum of money. She told me we could start looking for cash cars and I could use the money she gave me to buy it. Throwing the money in the air, I felt as if it were millions of dollars in my hand. We went around town searching for cash cars that didn't need much work. Finally, I came across one I liked. We pulled over to the side of the street and saw a man writing numbers on a car. I rolled my window down to speak to him.

"Hey, how you doing sir? How much is that car?"

"Hey, young lady. My name is Steve. Its $2,200. It's a 1990 Nissan Maxima. If you must get anything for it, it may just be a battery, radio, and starter. Everything else is fine. I'll even let you take it for a test-drive if you'd like."

"Alright, sure. Let me park and I'll be over shortly."

My mom and I got out of the car and walked over to the man. I proceeded to the driver side while my mother went to the back and the man on the passenger side. I started the car, pressed lightly on the gas, and strolled forward. Steve turned on the air to the highest temperature and it blew out like a strong wind from a storm. From the start to finish it was a smooth ride. I didn't hear any noise or feel anything unusual. Stepping out of the car, I gave it one more look. I opened the truck to see if it had a lot of space, a spare tire, and a jack. Luckily, everything was there and one less thing I had to worry about. I popped the lock to the hood of the car and checked the oils, the battery, and the wires.

"Mama should I go ahead, or should we keep looking?"

"Do you feel like it's not much work to be done? Hold on, let me call my insurance agency and see how much it would cost to add you on to my insurance. In my head, I thought to myself, I'm not sure. I hope this car is not a lemon. Is it worth the price he's asking for? It had no music, but I figured I could just use my phone. Thinking things over, I decided to get the car. However, since it does need some work done the price must come down.

"Due to the parts I will end up having to get for the car, can we negotiate to bring the price down?'"

"Alright, what are you thinking?"

"How about $1,900?"

"How about $2,000? Because see the retail price is really $3,550. So, I should be charging a little more."

"How about $1, 950?"

"Alright, sold, you got it. It's all yours. Here are the title and my number if you have any questions. Have a great day!"

As soon as I pulled up to the house my phone rang. I had been waiting on this call all day. "Look I can't do this anymore. You had a whole other female texting me off your phone, you stood me up for homecoming, you've been cheating, and your attitude is stank as fuck." I hung up the phone and entered the house. My mom asked me was I okay and I told her what happened. She gave me a pep talk and I went to my room, throwing my keys on my bed. It's like the more I got to know him, the more I realized my self-worth and the fact that I don't have to put up with his shit. Being the person that I was, I kept looking over it knowing that there was some good within him. It's like everybody saw him as a monster, but I saw him as a teddy bear who tried to be a soldier on the outside. I couldn't keep making excuses for him though.

Throughout the day he called me back to back. Like damn I couldn't understand why he didn't get the message that I did not want to be bothered with his ass. After our break-up, everybody asked me why the relationship didn't work and I would say it wasn't meant to be because I wanted people to stay out my business. It felt refreshing being single again. The school year was going great, goals were being accomplished, and work wasn't overwhelming.

Life seemed like it was actually getting on track. Days later, we traveled to Moss Point, Mississippi to pick up my dad. My dad and I relationship were progressing to the point where we talked almost every day. He was really showing that he cared and wanted to be a part of my life. On the other hand, as far as his relationship with my mom, it was best that they co-parent. Getting back to the house, we settled in to take our bath and eat. A couple of hours later my mentor, Mrs.Watkins, texted me that she had pulled up. I strutted downstairs to go welcome her in and see if she needed any help with her bags. Stepping out of her car, she reached out her arms for a hug. I was shocked that my mentor drove ten hours to see me graduate, but not only that to help bring my purpose out. Second, I felt like her Facebook profile picture was lying because she was extremely tall. She followed me into the house, greeted everyone, and went to go take her shower. While she was handling her hygiene, I began preparing for the next day. After she got dressed, we stayed up for a few hours talking each other heads off. "Alright, get some rest," I said making my way downstairs to the blow-up mattress. I put my phone on the charger and fell asleep. The sound of birds chirping woke me up and I let the air out of the air mattress.

I then went upstairs and knocked on the door, hearing movement from the outside of the door. She opened the door and I gathered my clothes and toothbrush and entered the bathroom. After taking care of my hygiene, I went downstairs to see what my mom cooked for breakfast. We ate and Mrs.Watkins offered to take me to my make-up appointment. Pulling up into the driveway, we got out and knocked on the door. I followed her into the basement and sat in the chair. After a few minutes, I looked into the mirror and gave her the money. She let me use her bathroom to change over into my graduation dress. We arrived back at the house and everybody was getting dressed, as it got closer and closer to the time for us to leave.

"Wow, baby girl you look like my mama," my daddy smiled. "I mean you don't need the make-up, but you look beautiful big mama." "Thanks, Daddy," I cheesed. As soon as everybody was done, we loaded up into our cars and headed to the ceremony. We pulled up into the parking lot and I got out to snap some pictures. After standing in the hot sun for minutes, I left the family to go find my spot in line. After all the speeches, it was finally my row's time to go on stage. "Next, we have Diana Baker-Boatwright..." Strutting across the stage, I smiled brightly over into the direction of where my folks were sitting. Everybody was smiling, waving, and cheering for me. I walked back to my seat waiting for my row to finish, so we could all sit. In no time, the hats were thrown in the air and we made our way back to where our families were catching up with friends. Traffic was packed as we made it back to the house. The next few days I split my time amongst my mentor and my dad hanging out, going out to eat, and my dad favorite activity…basketball.

Ch7 Heart Wants What the Heart Wants

Everybody was gone and now it was time to get back to work and prepare for college. One day I got a text from a number I didn't recognize saying, "Hey, how are you?" I text back, "who this?" "Listen please, It's Darius. I'm not saying we have to jump into a relationship, but I was wondering if you would give me a second chance." I was indecisive about the situation, so I told him that I would think about it. After hanging out and getting to know each other all over again, we ended up making it official. I must say it seemed like his attitude improved. This time I made it clear that it would be different and boundaries were to be put in place. A couple of mornings later, I took off my sleeping mask, letting the light hit my face. Rubbing my eyes, I got out of bed and entered the bathroom. Grabbing my toothbrush and turning on the radio, I brushed my teeth. I stepped in the tub and turned on the shower and pulled the shower curtain forward. I lathered up my towel as I sang and danced to the music.

Knock! Knock! "What do you need?" I yelled out. My sister on the other end of the door yelled she needed to brush her teeth. I yelled for her to come in and she brushed her teeth. I lathered my body with the Japanese Blossom Body wash.

My sister finished and left out to do whatever she was getting ready to do. I rinsed off my body and stepped out of the tub, pulling my towel from the rack. I slipped into my robe, cut off the radio, and went to my room to get dress. I picked out a white cut up shirt and ripped blue jean shorts from the closet. Lotioning up my body, I put on piece by piece. Then, I slid into my white diamond sandals and sprayed on some perfume. "Mama I'm gone," I yell out to my mother as I gathered my wallet, jacket, and keys. I locked the door behind me and headed to my car.

Putting on the seatbelt, I turned on the car and searched through my playlist to listen to a song while I drove. I pulled out the parking lot and drove over to Darius's house within minutes. After arriving at his house, I knocked on the door to see Darius in a white top, khaki shorts and sandals. He was so fine! "Awe babe, you look so cute," I said. "Thanks, you look good too." He smiled, shutting the door behind me. I went to sit down on the couch, while they finish getting ready. Getting settled in the car, he pulled into the kitchen to get gas and coffee. "Y'all need anything," he asked his sister and me. We told him we were good. Soon after we were on the highway with him driving mostly with the cruise control on. We stopped here and there for snacks and gas until we finally pulled up into his auntie's driveway.

He introduced me to everyone and then we started loading up the car to go to the baby shower. Stepping into the pink and blue decorated building, we got a seat and waited for the planner to tell us the activities. We played a few games and I won some Bath and Body Works Cherry Blossom Perfume. As we began fixing our plate, more family came in. After we ate, Darius, his sister, and I walked outside to get some air. Darius sister pulled out her phone and started snapping pictures of her brother and me. We went back inside and everybody had started cleaning, therefore, we cleaned up our area and got back on the road. We arrived back in town in no time. Unlocking the car, he pushed the button so his sister could go in the house. We talked for a bit and then he walked me over to my car. Leaning in, he kissed me and I grabbed his chin to get more kisses. He opened my door, as I got in to start up the car. He told me to text him when I made it home. After arriving back at home, I unlocked the door, tiptoed to the bathroom, showered, and slouched in my bed, and fell asleep.

On the first day of college, I woke up feeling like it was the first day of high school all over again. I had my mom take pictures of me before I went on my way. Arriving at Mississippi State, it was very straight-forward. You did your work, attended class, and stayed in your own lane. Everybody seemed so friendly, sometimes too friendly. In between classes, I would sit in my car to relax or go to the library to do homework so when I got home I didn't have to worry about staying up late at night. It was the last class of the day and I left there and went to the school's café. I got a sub and called to see what Darius was doing. Pulling up to his house, I got up and went to the door. I noticed it was slightly open, so I pushed it in. "Bae, where you at," I yelled out. "In the shower," I heard him say from the back. Going into his room, I laid my stuff on his dresser and laid on top of his bed and turned on the TV.

He came in the room with just his boxers on.

"I just got home from work. How was your first day?"

"It was good. Kind of felt like the first day of high school, but nothing I can't handle. How was your day?"

"My back has been hurting so bad lately, more than usual. Other than that, it was good."

"Bae, would you like me to give you a back massage?"

"Yeah, sure. The baby oil is on the dresser."

Putting on some shorts, he laid across the bed. Swinging my leg across the bed, I straddle over his lower back. I poured the baby oil in my hand and began to rub it onto his shoulders and down his back. "Bae, right there, go down," he said. "Don't be scared, you're not hurting me". I press deeper into his skin with my elbows. I massaged all over his shoulders. "Babe, that feels a lot better," he smiled. I put the baby oil back onto the dresser. Stepping into his house shoes, he walked over to his recliner. I went into the kitchen to wash my hands and get my food. "You want some?" I asked. He shook his head and went towards the kitchen. I laid back in his recliner and waited for him to come return. He came back with a plate of lasagna, mixed veggies, and garlic bread. After a while, we watched a bit of TV and talked, as I noticed it was getting darker and darker outside. Walking out to my car, I pulled my keys out of my pocket. Swinging a blue cord like can, he came walking outside. "Do you know where the reservoir is located for the air conditioner?" he asked. I open the hood of the car, so we could see if we could find it. I turn on the flashlight on my phone and within seconds, I found where it was located. He plugged the cord into the reservoir and began to pump the can. I turned on the car and let it run for a bit with the air turned on. It started to get cold and I was very excited. "Thanks for fixing the air babe!" I said. "No problems love, can't have you out here in this heat." He said. He slammed my hood down and watched me disappear into the distance.

The next morning, I woke up to dead silence and eventually remembered that everybody was gone to work or school. I took care of my morning hygiene and put on some clothes to go run some errands and see if I could get my car fixed. Locking up the house, I pushed the unlock button on the key alarm and got in. Turning down on the side street, my car started slowing down and I pulled over into a nearby church parking lot. It felt like my whole world came crumbling down. I called my mom to see what I should do, but she was at work. Tears start rolling down my face as I look down to scroll to my grandmother's number. I really didn't want to, but there was really no one else I could call. My grandmother answered her phone and told me that she would arrive shortly. About thirty minutes later, she arrived and I put my car in neutral so she could push my car into the street. She pushed me to the house. Thank God it wasn't far because I would have had to pay for a tow truck. I texted my mother and asked her to get me a bike after she got off work so that I could get from class to class. Two days later, I ended up buying a black charger from one of the car lots my grandmother knew. Ring! Ring! I look down at my phone to see Darius calling.

"Hey love, what are you up to?"

"Oh, nothing much, doing homework. What about you?"

"You need help with it? And I was wondering if you are doing anything important on Thursday?"

"No, I got it. Thanks for the gesture though. And remember I have to stay after school so that I can finish my group project. I'm free on Friday."

"You don't ever have time for me. You're messing around with one of those boys, aren't you?"

"First of all, lower your tone. Second, I always make time for you even with my busy schedule. But, do you do the same? If you're not free on Friday, we can go somewhere over the weekend. And you know damn well to be asking me that stupid ass question."

"Nope, I work on the weekend. And yeah okay, I'm busy too. It's whatever though."

"When did you start working on weekends? Nobody said that you aren't busy, but yeah okay."

"Don't worry about it. You act like school is your whole life. You don't know anything."

In the pit of my stomach, it felt like knots were forming. After all the back and forth, I felt like he was cheating. My intuition told me he was either talking to his ex-again or found someone new. If it was true, this would be the last straw. No more going in and out of my life when you want to and giving a stank ass attitude for no reason.

"Welcome to Burger King. Would you like to try our Sourdough King?"

"No thank you, may I get two iced coffees, please. Thank you."

Before I could even tell them their total, the car sped around the corner. I look over to collect the change, only to see that Darius was driving the car. He had his way of making me feel like he was sorry and trying to do better. He had his earphones in his ears as if he was talking on the phone. Passing him his drink, I looked over to see him wink his eyes and zoom off. It was getting close to the time of me getting off. I was so glad because some customers came in as if they woke up on the wrong side of the bed. Taylor, a cashier, came in to relieve me from my shift. She came over by me smiling, reaching for the headset. "You should go with my best friend. She thinks you are cute." She said. "I'm taken," I laughed, walking over to count my drawer down. I thought girls were attractive, but I wasn't about to step out on my boyfriend. Pulling out the lot, I called my mom to see what she cooked for dinner. I decided to go home instead of picking up food to eat. Coming through the door, the air was filled with the smell of fried chicken. "Your plate in the microwave," my mom yelled from upstairs. I went into the kitchen, grabbed my plate, and sat on the couch in the front room. I kicked my shoes off, laid back, and watched TV as I ate. I felt tiredness come over me. I head upstairs to shower and returned to my bed for school the next morning.

Pulling up into the parking lot, I checked my school's dashboard to look at my grades. I notice that my grade dropped in my Business Economics Class. I made a note in my phone to ask the teacher about it. I refused to let it ruin my day. I walked into my math class ready to be entertained by Mr. Lincoln's jokes. Time flew by the rest of the day. Next time I looked up, I was in my Business Class, while the teacher wrapped up the lecture. After she concluded I waited until everyone left and asked her about my grade. "There is nothing I can do. If you didn't sign the attendance sheet, then that's your problem." She rolled her eyes. "So, there's nothing I can do to prove to you that I was in your class or someone else I can talk to?" I said. "Nope. I have to go. Have a good one." She smirked and walked away. I was so blown away by her rudeness.

I met up with some friends at the lounge and explained to them what happened. Someone blurted out, "Oh that's just Professor White. She has her favorite students and she's also racist." "And nobody does anything about it huh?" I stated. Everybody started chiming in on their experience with different situations of racism at the school. After a while, I was irritated so I decided to ride up to Smoothie King and get a tropical berry smoothie. I pull up at my friend, Karen's house to give her the dye that I wanted in my weave. Suddenly, my phone was flooded with messages from Darius. Basically, the messages said that he thought we should break up and how much he didn't deserve to be with me. Something in my spirit told me that he was going to break up with me before I told him. Just like a coward, he couldn't tell me face to face. I was baffled by what he was saying, especially when he's talking heavily about the future, wanting to be my husband, having children, and all those other sweet lies. At the same time, I was relieved because I loved him, but I wasn't in love with him. That's not all, it seemed as if there was always a problem when it came to me talking about my goals.

My mom raised me to be independent, so I wouldn't dare to let him come in between me furthering my education. I told Karen I would hit her up later. I pull out the driveway and turned the corner to get on the main street. It seemed like after I broke up with him, girls and boys were hitting on me left and right. But let me run that back, I said GIRLS. Looking back at my religious background and judgmental family, there was no way I could even consider looking at a girl. My mom's parents were involved in the church a lot, especially since my mom's dad was a preacher. Also, growing up around Grandma Mary, she made it very clear that she did not support other relationships other than ones that were heterosexual. If you were anything other than heterosexual, you were considered "wrong, confused, or nasty". I figured, if she felt that way, then all her children did, too. So, for a long time, I felt compelled to not end up in a lesbian relationship. I pulled into Chevron gas station and those feelings went away when I ran into an old friend, Ciara.

"Hey Diana, how have you been?"

"Good, back and forth between school and working. How about you?"

"Same. I'm actually about to head to work, now. Here's my number. Let's catch up."

"Okay, bet. Have a good day."

Smiling like a kid in the candy store, I took the paper and slid it into my pocket. I couldn't believe that fine ass Cira gave me her number. We were cool back in middle school, but we weren't around each other much because we only had P.E together. Letting a couple of days pass by, I decided to give her a call. Digging into my jacket pocket, I pulled out the piece of paper and dialed the digits.

"Hey, CeeCee. This is Diana. How are you and the family?"

"We're good. I'm just trying to make sure I'm picking the right major and trying not to go off on some of my co-workers at my job. But you know how that goes. Family is still being their crazy selves and what about you and yours?"

"Family is the same as yours. That's good to hear. I suggest that if it's not what you really want to do change it. And man, these jobs are something else. I'm dealing with this racist and high demanding tuition school. Other than that life is good."

"Yeah, I'll figure it out. Girl, you're smart. I know you can push through. Do you still go with Darius?"

"Right into the questions, huh? But, no to answer your question. Anybody swept you off your feet yet?"

"More like swept over me."

"You're messing with the wrong ones."

"Yeah, whatever."

We talked until the sun came up like we knew each other for years. It was something about her that just made the vibe so matched. But I didn't want to seem too straightforward or thirsty. I woke up to music playing in my mom's room. And everybody knew what that meant---clean up time. So, I sunk deeper into my bed, trying to hide under the pillow. She then pushed the vacuum into my room. "I know you are not sleeping. Go ahead and get up and start cleaning," she said. I went ahead and got up to take care of my hygiene first. Then, I came back to my room to make up my bed. Ciara was on my mind, but I didn't want to overstep any boundaries, so I decided not to call her. As soon as I cleaned off my dresser, I heard a beep from my phone. It was from Ciara asking me what I was doing. Letting some time pass by, I texted her back that I was cleaning up. I grabbed the vacuum and went across my floor a couple of times and then I went downstairs to do the dishes. Dishes seem like they would take forever. And I hated when people didn't rinse their bowls or left food out and I had to be the one to get it out. Finishing up the dishes, I grabbed a Dr. Pepper and headed back to my room. Grabbing my phone, I saw that I had two missed calls from Ciara. I laid on top of my bed and facetime her.

"What's up? About time you answered the phone."

"Nothing, just about to chill and do some things on my laptop. Girl, I told you I was cleaning."

"Mmhm. You were probably over at Darius house. Have you heard J Cole's new album?

"I'm going to need you to stop bringing up Darius. You bring him up more than I do. You should go with him then. And yep I listened to it."

"HAHA, dang you don't have to get an attitude. I was just playing. What has got your panties in a bunch?"

"Yeah okay Darius's girlfriend. I'm about to go get me something to eat. I'll talk to you later."

I really wasn't going to get food. I just said that to get off the phone. She was the only one who knew how to work my nerves. Like damn girl chill. I called it a day and watched TV until I fell asleep. My alarm went off for me to get up for work. I got up, showered, dressed, and headed to work. The best part about having a morning shift is the day seemed to go by fast and then I got the rest of the day to do what I wanted. I walked in through the doors and clocked in. Flicking the switch, the rest of the lights came on. I hit all the buttons for the appliances to warm up. I went over to the sink and washed my hands. Then I walked to the back and brought all the food out the pantry to start prepping for breakfast. My manager was over in the office counting down the drawer. The sun began to rise and customers began pouring in like rain. "Hey, sweetie," one of the regular customers said to me while I put the food on the hot chute. I waved and continued to fix the food that was popping up on my screen. Time went by and I then began prepping for lunch so the next person who came in could transition smoothly. By the time I clocked out, I felt my phone vibrating in my pocket. Ciara and I were talking every day on the phone from sunup to sundown.

"Hello, what's up?"

"What are you doing? I'm hungry."

"Just got off work. Tired as hell and me too."

"Are you going to get something to eat? If so, come get me."

"Yeah and let me go shower first."

"Yeah okay, stinky."

"I do not stink. Where are we going to eat?"

"Hmmm. I don't know."

"Alright, bet. I'm going to surprise you."

"I do not like surprises, so go ahead and tell me now."

"Bruh, you so picky dang.

"Okay, I'm not going then."

"I want some Wingstop. Their wings are so good, bruh. And those fries be hitting."

"Yeah, ok. I'll try it. Let me go fix my hair."

"Who are you trying to get cute for?"

"Your brother."

"Girl, don't play with me."

By this time, I made it home and got in the shower. Working at a food place can be so damn tiring. I brushed my teeth, went to my room to lotion up, and get dressed. Grabbing some gum, I put it in my pocket. I told my mom I was about to go. "Alright, be safe." She said. I cranked up the car, put it in reverse, and zoomed into the direction of the main road. Her parent's house was a hop and skip away. Pulling up into her parent's driveway, I got out the car and knocked on the door. Her mom opened it and asked if I wanted anything to drink. I declined and sat down on the couch in the living room. We talked for a bit until I heard Ciara come from the back. "Hey, you can come to the back," she said. I got to her room and sat at the end of the bed. She started looking around for her shoes opening the closet and scamming the floor. Finally, she found them underneath her bed. Her dad came in and greeted me. His hand had the grip of a lawyer that's been working over forty years. As he exited the room, he closed the door. I rubbed my hand to get the tension out. Ciara laughed at me, "You can't take a handshake." "You see the way he shook my hand," I said, "He got my hand numb." "Girl nothing's wrong with you," she said." Let's go." With my keys in my hand, I led the way out to my car. I pulled out of the driveway with the music blasting and drove up to Wingstop.

I got out and held the door open for her to walk in. We ordered our food and sat down at the table in the corner. She bumped into my foot underneath the table. "What you trying to do, play footsies?" I laughed. She rolled her eyes, "Girl nobody was trying to do nothing." I loved messing with her on purpose. The server brought us our food and we dug in with the quickness. Barbeque sauce fell on her titty and she got a napkin and wiped it off. Food was disappearing off our plates like we were in a magic show. I was down to three wings when I looked up and saw she had finished her whole plate. "Damn, I guess I'm a slow eater," I said. "Yeah you are," she snickered. We got up and threw our trash away. She went to the bathroom, while I filled up our drinks. Walking to the car, she tried to trip me up. But I caught her just in time for me to go around. I hated that I had to go the work the next day. But I didn't mind spending time with her, even if it was just to sit in silence. That's how much I liked having her in my company. But somehow, I couldn't get the courage to ask her out. I wanted to go to the movies, but she convinced me to save our money and watch a movie at her crib. I pulled up into her driveway and she pulled out her key to get us in the house. Following her to her room, I sat on the edge of the bed. "Diana, you want to try the tea I made?" Ciara asked. Her mama walked past and said, "I wouldn't try that nasty ass tea if I were you." She had me laughing so hard that I couldn't breathe. "Ain't nothing wrong with my tea." CeeCee laughed. "You trying to make me have the booboo guts at your house?" I asked, "Nope, not today." She laughed and turned on Netflix, searching through to find us a movie. Finally, she found one that she hasn't seen. I mean I thought I was a movie fanatic. It seemed like every movie I wanted to watch she had already seen. We laid in the bed with the fan on max. The movie started getting good and here she goes trying to play around. She swatted me with her pillow. The movie was still playing while we wrestled. I almost pushed her off the bed, but I caught her. "Dang, you got muscles," she said. "I do workout, remember," I said. Dun! Dun! The movie came to the end and that was my cue that it was time to go. Especially, since I had work the next day. "Text me when you make it home," she said. I pulled off into the darkness and made my way home, dodging the high-beam lights that were passing me by. I made it to the house, and everybody was counting sheep, you would have thought it was a farm in the house. I called Ciara to tell her I made it and we started up a whole conversation. I was getting sleepy and fell asleep on her. ZZzz!

All of a sudden, I felt like I was getting too much sleep. I didn't hear my alarm go off, so I quickly jumped up. I looked at the time and I had 25 minutes to get to work. I brushed my teeth and got dressed within ten minutes. I pulled into the parking lot in no time. The opener and I pulled up at the same time. "Girl I'm so tired," the manager said, "Are you ready to get this day over with?" "Girl yeah," I said. We talked as we prepared for the day. I dropped the basket of sausages into the grease. I started thinking about Ciara and ways I could ask her out, but she didn't like surprises. I snapped out the daydream when I heard the alarm going off for the sausages. Letting the grease drain off, I pulled the basket and put them in the designated tray. My manager came by and did a count on the food. Beep! The timer on the biscuits went off and I went to go pull them out of the oven. A customer walked up, "Good Morning, I want two sausage biscuits and a cup of coffee." My manager took his order and made small talk with him. I quickly bagged the food and placed it on the counter. Time started speeding up and customers started rushing in. One of the other employees called off at the last minute causing us to be short-handed. The manager and I were running around like chickens with our head cut off. I was so ready to get off. It was becoming tiresome that every time I worked, employees were calling out left on right. As soon as the next person walked in the back to get on the board, I hauled ass to clock out. My time was past-due, my feet felt like a swollen potato, and my stomach was growling loud like a dog at a stranger.

Getting in the car, I turned on the air and put my seatbelt on. I turned in behind the traffic of cars that passed by. So many things were on my mind, so I turned on the radio to erase my thoughts. I passed by two wrecks before I made my way to the house. You would think people got their licensed revoked the way they drove. I got through the door and my mom was on the couch braiding up my sister's hair. Going into the kitchen, I fixed a plate of food and something to drink. I walked back into the living room and watched TV with them, while they were occupied with hair. "You had a good day at work?" my mom said. "Yeah, it was fine," I told her. I didn't want to stress her about work because it really just seemed like a part of life, in having a difficult job. It was just something you had to suck up and deal with. I finished my plate and put my dishes away. Going upstairs, I picked out some pajamas and went running some bath water. I poured a cap of blossom bubble bath into the hot, running water. I turned on the music to my favorite playlist and got undressed. After soaking for a couple of minutes, I got dressed and went into my room. I turned on my TV and Pandora was still on the screen. It was playing "Body Party by Ciara" and my mind raced back to the time Ciara and I was in the car and that same song was on. I felt like I was really starting to fall in love with her. I knew we weren't together, but to feel a connection so strong with someone was something you don't pass by often, if at all. Bad thoughts were floating through my mind and I began to question my feelings. I thought, should I follow my heart and go after her or should I just let it be? The school was aggravating me and I couldn't figure out if I was taking the right major or should I move on to another school. Getting on my knees at the edge of my bed, I put my hands together and prayed to God.

"Dear God,

I come before you as humble as I know how. Lord, I want to thank you for everything that you do and everything that you continue to do. Even if you never do anything else for me, you have done enough. But I know you won't stop because your love lasts for eternity. I pray for my family, friends, enemies, and everybody across the world. Please forgive me for my sins. I ask that you continue to pour your love upon me, guide me, strengthen me, and that I draw closer to you. Please give me a sign, to show me what decision I need to make for school. Lord I know sometimes I fall, but I know you are right there to carry me. I feel like there's something wrong with me. I am attracted to girls and I can't seem to understand why. Will I really go to hell, if I feel this way? Can I pray it away? Will you stop loving me because of how I feel? Can you please show me a sign that I'm going the wrong way? Lord, I don't want to lose you. Please help me. I love you so much. In the name of Jesus, I pray, Amen."

I got in my bed and tears slid down my face, as I closed my eyes to sleep. The next morning, I got up and made myself some breakfast. After I finished eating,

I sat at the kitchen table and made a list of pros and cons of being at the school. I wrote out a plan to get to where I needed to be. Looking intently through my notes and praying continuously, I made my final decision. I showered, got dressed quickly, and picked up my keys off the dresser. I walked up to the business office and tapped the bell. A lady walked over to the window and started to assist me.

"How may I help you?"

"I would like to withdraw and send my transcript over to two schools I'm interested in transferring to."

"And what is your reason for leaving?"

"I feel as if my journey here is over. I believe God is wanting me to go elsewhere."

"No, like is it because the tuition is too high, you can't afford it, or you don't like a certain program."

"I just explained it to you."

"Well, okay."

I filled out the information I needed for her to send off my transcripts. The feeling the came over my body when I turned to leave and go home was the feeling I usually get when I do the right thing. I knew at that very moment that I was on the right path. If going to this college was not going to get it, another opportunity is always on the other side. Pulling up to my house, I felt exhausted. I laid on the couch, listening to the fan blow and occasional chirps here and there. My eyes slowly closed and I found myself dreaming about Ciara. One thing led to another as I found myself with just a sports bra on and dripping wet at the core. Grabbing her hair softly, I pull it to the back so it could stay out of her face. Her tongue moved like a snake the way she went in and out making me wetter and wetter. She had me in tsunami mode. I tried so hard not to bust but what can I say the baby was putting in that work for real! Sliding two fingers in me really fast, she licked my center ever so softly. Her tongue went deeper and deeper as she took on all my juices. Looking into my eyes, she licked her fingers. That's when I lost it and went down to kiss her soft plump lips, grabbing her ass all at the same time. Taking off her tank top, I began to suck on her tits, leaving hickeys all over them. I slightly removed her shorts, kissing her inner thighs as I caressed her beautiful, perky breast. Moving over to her clit, I start off with fast strokes of my tongue and then I slowed it down going in and out of her pussy as I felt her grip on me tighten. Her legs trembled. Ciara moaned, "D, I'm finna cum." "Nah baby, hold that shit," I said. She pulled my hair as I felt her body twitching beneath me. "Look at me Cee," I whispered as I felt her release her juices all over my chin. Suddenly, I woke up looking around the living room to breathe. "Damn, it was a dream," I said to myself. I haven't been hearing from Ciara lately, so I decided to check up on her.

"Hey, did I do or say something wrong?"

"No, what are you talking about?"

"I just feel like your vibe has been off, lately."

"I've been acting the same way. I don't know what you're talking about."

"So, you don't think that you've been a little distant lately."

"No, I haven't. You're tripping. All I've been doing is hanging with my family."

"Yeah, okay. Well, that's all you had to say?"

"Girl, whatever. I'll talk to you later."

Hanging up the phone, I thought about the argument we just had. I paced the floor back and forth on whether I should call her and apologize, but I didn't know why I would be doing it. I just wanted to express my feelings to her. Well, I guess I'll just give her some space and see if she calls back. Getting comfortable under the sheets, I laid on my back staring at the ceiling. Weeks went by and I decided to look up her profile on Instagram and clicked on the first picture that popped up. Swiping to the left, I saw a picture of her kissing some girl. Damn! My heart started beating faster than usual and I was at a loss of words. Looking at the caption, I read, "Me and Bae living our best life." I felt like somebody ripped out my heart, cut it up, and tried to place it back in my body, only to find out it will no longer beat. I shook my head looking at the pictures, thinking to myself," I'm too late. I should've admitted how I truly felt." The one person who I really wanted and dreamed of spending the rest of my life with was now booed up with someone else. After experiencing that, I felt like I wasn't meant for relationships at all. Like maybe, I was the reason why I couldn't be in a relationship with someone.

At that moment, I felt like I was beginning to lose myself. I didn't know if I wanted a bowl of ice cream or Keyshia Cole songs on replay to soothe me. The next couple of days it was hard to not hear from her or see her anymore. After drowning in my sorrow for what seemed like an eternity, I decided to get in the gym. I figured the gym was always a way of relieving stress. Months went by with a new and improved Diana. I was feeling better and looking better. No more for feeling sad about "would've, should've, could've". It was time to move on to what the future held. Just because that didn't work out doesn't mean I won't be able to find love again, maybe even better love. After my workout, I went to go shower that sweat off. Moisturizing my skin, I put on some clothes and went to go get a poster board out of my supply space. I picked up a journal and wrote some small term and long-term goals that I wanted to accomplish and ended up with 20 goals. I picked up my suitcase and pulled out my laptop. Opening it, I typed in my password and click on google to look up some pictures to represent for the twenty goals and pasted it to Microsoft Word. I went downstairs, hearing the sign of beeping, to catch the papers that were being printed off. I went back into my room, cut out the pictures, and pasted them to the board. Each time I knock out a goal I would sign and date it. It seemed like the more goals I would put up the more goals were getting finished. Finishing up, I placed the board in the corner of my room. I was so excited, dancing all the way downstairs, I went into the kitchen and fixed me a bowl of fruit. I guess reading those self-empowerment books were really paying off. It was shifting my whole mindset.

"Dinner's ready," my mom yelled down from the kitchen. They say the best way to a man heart is food. But I like to think different. Anytime food is involved I am all mouth. I went downstairs and fixed my plate. Everybody was chilling in their own zone, so we decided to eat in our rooms. I poured me a glass of Root Beer and carried my plate back to the room. I turned on Netflix and turned to a comedy movie. Before I dug in, I prayed:

Dear God,

Thank you for simply being here for me. Thank you for waking me up this morning and giving me another day to live out your purpose. Thank you for continuing to put food on my plate. Thank you for my mom cooking this great food. Thank you for not giving up on me, even when I was giving up on myself. I just want to say thank you for loving me unconditionally, everything you do, and I couldn't have a better father than you. Please continue to cover me and guide me. Thank you in advance for what you have ahead for me. Oh yeah, thank you for accepting me. In Jesus name, I pray. Amen.

Ch8 Can you be my baby girl?

Coming into Lakeside Mall, I spotted this slim-thick, bright green-eyed, light-skinned girl with long hair leaving Victoria Secret. Damn, she was fine. From afar I could see that her ass was fat as a plum poking out her pants. She had some friends walking with her too. But my eyes couldn't help but give her all the attention. I went into Footlocker looking for some shoes for my brother's birthday. He told me about some new Jordan's that were coming out. I picked up some puma socks and found me and my brother the same pair of shoes he was talking about. Checking out at the register, I noticed the same beautiful ass girl from earlier was passing by. Walking over to the group of ladies, I smiled trying to figure out what I was going to say. *Clears Throat* "Hey beautiful, may I get your number, so I can see you sometime?" Her girlfriends nudging her and telling her to say yeah. Putting my number in her phone, in a soft voice, she says, "maybe, I'll think about it." "I'll be waiting," I replied with a wink and walked away. I can tell baby-girl seemed a little shy, but she just doesn't know I'm a woman who goes after EVERYTHING I want in life. Pulling off in my blue 2019 Ford Mustang, I dropped by my mom's house to grab a plate to eat.

Today, she cooked steak, twice-loaded baked potatoes, steamed broccoli, and sweet corn on the cob. Man, when I tell you moms be in the kitchen. She stays in that thang! "So, what you got going on?" she asked. "I went by Footlocker today and got me and my brother a pair of shoes, but don't tell him," I said. We make small conversation and then I left to go to my apartment. I pulled up in the driveway and jogged my way into the bathroom. I had to pee so bad. After flushing the toilet, I washed my hands and went into the room to get out my pajamas. I quickly took a shower, put on my pajamas, and went to sleep.

A week has gone by and I still haven't heard a word from the girl I met at the mall. She didn't give me a name or anything. I'm in the gym room of my apartment complex running on the treadmill. I love exercising early in the morning. I think it's a good way to start my day off and it helps relax my mind. "Big Bank" is booming through my earphones. A lady walks in with a mat in her hand and rolls it out across the floor. I increase the speed on the treadmill and run faster. It started going too fast, so I slowed it down and took a sip of my Gatorade that was sitting on the side. Picking up my sweat towel, I dabbed it onto my forehead. I could feel the girl that came in from earlier staring at me, but I didn't pay her any mind. I got back to my apartment and took a shower. Throwing on some clothes, I walked outside to my car and headed up the street to McDonald's.

"Welcome to McDonald's, would you like to try our number two combo today?"

"No thank you, can I have a sausage McGriddle, hash brown, and a large vanilla iced coffee."

"Alright that total is $7.11. Pull forward to the second window, please."

"Okay, thank you."

I pulled up to the second window and give the lady my credit card. She opened the window, gave it back to me, and passes over my food and drink. I drove off pulling back into the driveway of my apartment. Going over to the living room, I cut on the TV to watch some news while I ate my food. I should have bought two iced coffees because they are just that good, I thought to myself. Today, was my off day, so I didn't need to worry about emails or none of that. I grabbed my phone and started scrolling on Facebook. Ding! I get a text from Christopher asking if I was at the crib. I shot him a text telling him he can pull through. Knock! Knock! I peeped through the peephole and opened the door.

"What it do?"

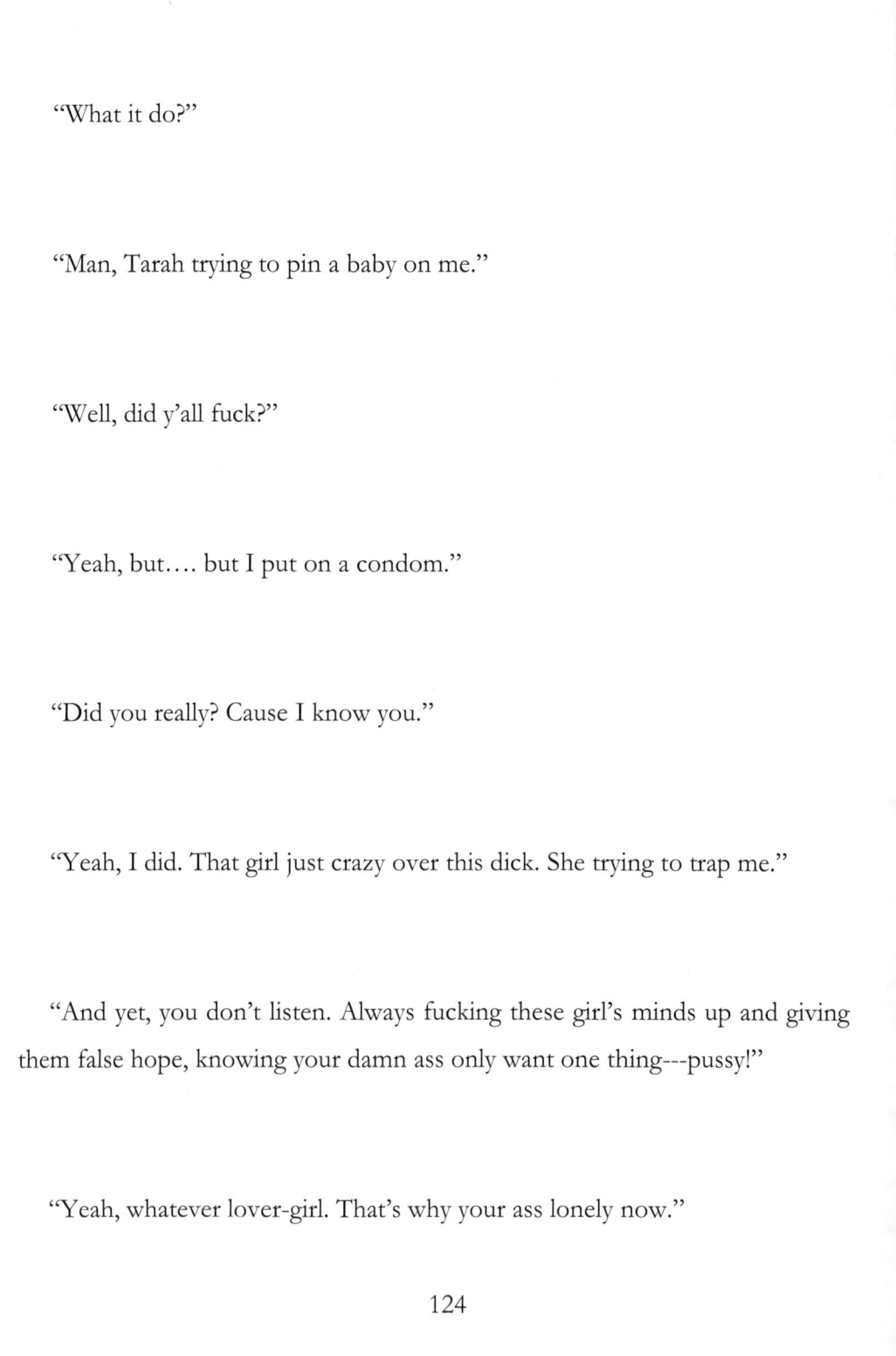

"Man, Tarah trying to pin a baby on me."

"Well, did y'all fuck?"

"Yeah, but…. but I put on a condom."

"Did you really? Cause I know you."

"Yeah, I did. That girl just crazy over this dick. She trying to trap me."

"And yet, you don't listen. Always fucking these girl's minds up and giving them false hope, knowing your damn ass only want one thing---pussy!"

"Yeah, whatever lover-girl. That's why your ass lonely now."

"Sorry not sorry, for making sure I don't end up with an STD. And I'm not lonely pussy boy!"

"Shut up and come on so I can whoop your ass in 2K."

I walked over to the TV and hooked the cords to the back of the Xbox. Pressing the button for it to open, I placed the disc into the console and grabbed one of the controllers. We got into the second quarter and decided to take a break. I walked into the kitchen and grabbed us two bags of chips and two root beers. I'm scrolling through Facebook looking at different memes running down my timeline. Finishing up his drink, Christopher asked if I'm ready to finish the game. Playing the game can get serious sometimes, but today we were chill. This time we made a bet that whoever wins get $100. The score was 82-77 with Chris being the winner. Of course, he started running his mouth talking about he the "King of 2K". "Alright, time to pay up," he said. Laughing, I walked to my room to retrieve the money to give it to him. He began flexing and waving the money in my face. "Damn bruh, you act like you have never seen a hundred-dollar bill before," I said. "Don't get mad cause you lost. I'm out of here anyway and call me when you ready for the next ass whooping," he said. We laughed as he walked out the door and I shut and locked it behind him.

I went into the bathroom to run some hot water and put some bubble bath in it. Stepping out of my clothes, I reached under the sink to get some Epsom Salt. Cutting the water off, I made sure it was not too hot and then soaked in the water for about fifteen minutes. I lathered up my body, rinsed off, and got out the tub. Looking behind the bathroom door, I pulled down my robe and put it on. I had a taste for ice cream, so I went into the kitchen and scooped some ice cream into a cup and poured the leftover root beer that I had from earlier into the cup. I dropped in a spoon and straw and went back to my room. Pulling back the sheets, I got underneath the covers and turned on the TV to watch Martin. Rubbing my eyes, I rolled over and dozed off. I started dreaming that I walked into the doctor's office and the doctor told me that I was pregnant. "How far along am I?" I asked. Ring! Ring! Waking from the dream, I peeped over at my phone to see an unfamiliar number pop up. "Hello," I said in my sleepy voice. At first, I just heard breathing but then I heard someone say, "hey, it's me Nique from the mall, sorry I didn't mean to wake you."

"Oh, hey beautiful you're good, how was your day?"

"It was good."

"So, what about it that made it good?"

"Why you all up in my business?"

"I'm just trying to get to know you better, miss I don't give out all the details."

She started giggling and we started asking each other questions to get to know each other a little better. We were talking to each other all night all the way into the next morning. It seemed like we have known each other for forever. The vibe between us seemed so real and positive. She's so goofy and fine. But I couldn't wait to get to know her on a deeper level. Finishing up the call, we made an agreement that I would come to pick her up later that night at eight to go to Briquettes Steakhouse. I got up, went into the bathroom and did my morning hygiene. Stepping into my closet, I looked around to pick out my two outfits (one for right now and one for later tonight). I walked into the shower lathered up quickly and came out to dry off. I threw on my black and pink Nike jumpsuit and stepped into my Nike slides. I checked to make sure my baby, Princess was fed and had her water in her cage. "Watch the house for me and be a good girl while mommy's gone. I'll bring you back a big treat." I talked to Princess as if she could understand what I am saying. "Good morning D", my nosy neighbor Mrs. Rose said. "Hey," I replied as if I'm not interested as to what she had to say. I hopped in the car and got about five miles away from the house and stop at Flowerama.

I walked in and picked out some beautiful blue roses and tulips. Nique's favorite color is blue just like mine. "This must be for one lucky mother," the clerk said. "Ah, not quite, more like soon to be girlfriend," I replied blushing. I know I wanted to make baby girl my wife someday, but I didn't want to rush things so soon. I wanted to make sure that we were both on the same page and I think tonight will be a great start. I left the flower shop and went to Taco-Bell to get the new Caramel Apple Slushy. I called up my homeboy, Christopher. He told me about how he was ready to settle down and all that extra stuff. In the back of my mind, I laughed because I knew that this man was not ready for that. He has been a playa from the Himalaya ever since he came out the womb. "Bruh, you don't want to ever go out," he said. "Cause I'm busy tonight and you know I work a lot," I said. "Oh, I see how it is." He said. Wrapping up the conversation, I pulled into the parking lot of my office. I walked in and greeted my receptionist, Mrs. Hobbs. She was a sweet 30-year-old lady, had two kids, and was doing the damn thing. "You can take the rest of the day off. How're things going with Nyla?" I asked. "She's doing much better. The doctor said she must take her antibiotics." she replied. We talked more about her personal life and the business aspect of our Ministry. So far everything was looking good on our end. I really thank God that he introduced me to her because she was a blessing to me just as I was to her. She keeps our TWeen Queen Empowering Sisterhood Ministry intact.

Walking into the back, I closed my office door and watched the security cameras to make sure Mrs. Hobbs made it to her car safely. She pulled off into the distance leaving me with pure silence. Looking at my desktop, I saw there were emails that needed a reply. I scattered through that and got on to remove the paperwork off my desk. I'm at my last bit of paperwork when I glanced at my watch seeing that it is 6:45pm. Rushing out the door, I had my keys ready, so I could lock the doors. I hopped in the whip and did 60 mph all the way home. I couldn't help but smile knowing that I was going to see baby-girl again tonight. I showered and got dressed within minutes and headed back out the door. "Nique, I'll be pulling up in ten minutes," I told her. "Okay, baby." She says. I clenched my teeth and hung up. I met this girl literally just like a week ago and she was already giving me butterflies in my stomach. Man, I have never felt like this before. She's got to be the one I said to myself as I pulled up at the red light. I made a left and turned into Nique's driveway. I saw the lights turned off in the house and I figured she was getting ready to come out. I grabbed the flowers and hid them behind my back as I walked up to the porch. Out stepped Nique in a beautiful red and white lace dress. She was breathtakingly gorgeous. She cleared her throat, while I stared at her, and came down onto the porch. "Oh, my bad, but you look really beautiful baby," I complimented her. "You are looking pretty sexy yourself," she smiles hitting me in my chest. I almost dropped the flowers that I seemed to forget. "These are for you," I said. She sniffed the flowers and told me how beautiful they were. I took her by the hand and led her to the passenger side. Before I shut the door, I made sure she was all the way in and I took the flowers and put them in the backseat. I slid into the car and look both ways before backing out of the driveway. I could feel her looking at me while I drove. I glanced over, and she turned her head as if she wasn't looking. "You like what you see over here?" I asked. "Yeah, I do." She said biting her lip. Our flirting game was too strong. It was a comfortable silence as we pulled into the parking lot. I got out and went over to the passenger side and helped Nique out the car. I wasn't really a booty person, but she had a nice booty.

"Table for two," I told the clerk. He pointed at a table in the back of the restaurant. Just where I wanted to be, so we could focus on each other. We walked to the back of the restaurant and I pulled out her seat for her. We're at the table looking over the menu. The waitress came over and asked if we knew what we wanted to drink. Baby said she would have a Sprite and I told her for me I would have an iced tea with lemon. Then, she proceeded to ask if we needed a few more minutes to figure out what we were going to eat. Of course, we told her we do. The waitress walked away and tended to her other duties.

"This place you picked out, NaNa, is so beautiful."

"Thank you beautiful. I was hoping you would like it."

"Have you been here before?"

"Yeah, I've been here before for a friend's birthday party."

"Oh ok, I think I want the Filet Mignon Dinner with a side of sautéed mushrooms and onions. What are you getting?"

"Umm, I got a taste for some seafood. So, I will get the Chargrilled Oyster Dinner."

By this time, the waitress had come back with our drinks, and we placed our order. Leaving the waitress to collect our menu boards and disappearing into the back. "Baby, I'm going to the ladies room. I'll be right back," she said getting up and walking across the room. I heard a man say "She fine as fuck" from across the room. I laugh to myself because she was just that---fine! Everything was going great. The waitress came back and placed our plates on the table. "If you need anything give me a holler." She stated. She came back and sat down, took a napkin and placed it across her lap. "Baby give me your hands," I said. She places her hands over mine, as I closed my eyes, I began to pray over our food. "Lord we come before you today to thank you for the nourishment that is going into our bodies. Thank you for waking us up, for the cook who cooked the food, and for our daily bread in Jesus name we pray. Amen." Nique opens her eyes smiling brightly with her pearly white teeth and sexy plumped lips. "Time to dig in," baby exclaimed. With that being said, we were both digging into our plates within seconds. Between bites of our food, we talked about how our day went and how our families are. The waitress came over to check on us and refilled our drinks. Looking over at her plate, she still had quite a bit to go; however, I was very close to being done. I would make jokes here and there and she would just die laughing. I sipped on the last bit of my tea and slithered my tongue around in my mouth to feel for any food that was stuck in my teeth. "Check please," I said. The waitress came over to the table and put the receipt on the table. Baby and I reached for it. "I got it, Nique," I said. I hand the waitress over the money and told her to keep the change for her tip.

Nique and I dashed out the door and into the car. We put on our seatbelts and I headed towards the interstate. Popping in some gum, I turned on the radio to 93BLX. That station was always jumping. I looked over to see baby dancing in her seat. I'm singing the words to the song right along with the radio. I heard my phone beeping with notifications, but I ignored it knowing it wasn't anything important. I pulled over to the gas station, walked in to get wild berry skittles, and to pay for the gas. Before I pumped the gas, I passed the skittles over to baby. I peeped at her watching our surroundings as I got back into the car. "These are my favorite skittles. They're so sweet and juicy." I said. "I know something else that's sweet and juicy," she said as she licked her lips slowly. "Oh really, let me find out," I said. She rubbed her hand up and down my arm, as I turned the corner to her house. I slowly pulled into her driveway not wanting her to leave me. But I knew she probably had work or something to attend to tomorrow. We got to the door and she told me what a wonderful night she had. She stepped up on the porch and kissed me right on the lips about three times. Her kisses were soft as silk sheets. She stepped back into her house and pulled me by the hand. She stepped out of her heels and walked up to the stairs. Don't get me wrong, I wanted to have sex with her. Not just sex though, I wanted to actually make love to her body. I sat on the couch waiting for her to come down. She came back down with white lingerie on and a furry white robe. She pointed her fingers at me to come over to her. Speechless, I got up and she took her hand and placed it on mine and rubbed it over her body. Her frame was like an hourglass and she placed my hands over her booty. Leaning in, she kisses me while I grabbed her ass. "Let's stop baby." I stutter in and out of kisses. I saw a tear come down her face. "Baby, it's not that I don't want this, but I want to make sure we are taking our time and that it's a special moment for us both," I explain. She nodded as she turned around and I slightly grab her bringing her back into my arms kissing her on the forehead. We walked over into the living room and she pulled the couch out turning it into bed form. Using the remote, she turned on the TV and found us a good movie to watch. I took off my clothes leaving me in my panties and sports bra. Nique cuddled up next to me as she pulled the cover over both of us. I wrapped my arm around her as I rubbed her booty and she suddenly fell asleep on my chest. I kissed her forehead, cut off the TV, and laid back to fall asleep.

Ch 9 It's Either Now or Never

Today is the day I asked Nique to be my girlfriend. We have been talking for about three months now. I had the hotel room ready, so everything was in place I just had to go get Nique. She was at the house putting on her makeup last time I checked. I texted her to see if she was done, so I could pick her up. Ding. A message popped up saying, "I'm ready Pookie". I smiled knowing that this day should go as smooth as it possibly could. I pulled up to her driveway and knocked on the door. Nique kisses me and I directed her to the passenger side. "Baby, you know you don't have to open the door for me every time," said Nique. "I know baby, but you're my Queen so it's only right." I smiled. We pulled up at Municipal Park and before she walked off, I told her to wait, so I could get something from the trunk.

I took out the picnic basket and blanket. "Awe baby, this is so romantic," Nique blushed. Walking over to the freshly cut green grass, I laid out the sheet and opened the picnic basket. I poured her and myself a glass of Red Sparkling Wine. "Baby, you never fail to amaze me. I must be the luckiest woman in the world. What did I do to deserve all of this?" She asked looking into my eyes. "For simply bringing me genuine happiness, honesty, knowledge, loyalty, love, attention, support, care, understanding, sacrifice, and so much more. Nique, you deserve this and more. I can't wait to make you Mrs. Baker-Boatwright someday," I said. She got up and sat in my lap. I opened the basket and pulled out the parfait. Nique loved yogurt and fruit. I fed it to her and of course, she wanted to start getting freaky. "Uh," Nique fake moans. "Baby, you want to go feed the birds," I asked laughing and pointing at the water where the birds were swimming at. She got up and pulled her pants up adjusting her clothes. I smacked her on the ass and got up to adjust my clothes. I picked up the trash, threw it away, and gather the picnic basket. Nique picked up the blanket, shakes it out, and fold it.

We walked over to the car and put the items in and got the bread to feed the birds. Tearing off a piece of the bread, I threw it in the air and Nique ran to the other side, dramatically, as if she was getting attacked by them. She threw a piece of bread at me and the birds started flying in my direction. I ran towards her direction and we both just died laughing. I hugged her and plant kisses all over her face. By this time, we were both walking back to the car. Nique came out of nowhere and smacked me on my ass. "Bruh, stop it," I said. "You know you like it. Your booty, but my property," she said. "Bae, can you stop at the hair store? I need some glue," she asked. "Anything for my baby," I replied. I pull over to Beauty and Beyond and I saw my ex coming out. The same ex who dumped me because she got caught cheating. Nique walked into the store and I stayed in the car to make a phone call. "Is everything set and ready to go? Alright, great, we'll be there shortly." I hung up. Nique came back to the car.

"Did you see that girl staring me down?" she asked.

"Yeah baby, that's just an ex of mine. She doesn't want any problems. You have nothing to worry about, besides you're my gain. That's her loss."

"Oh okay, because she was about to get these hands looking all stank."

Winding up the windows, I couldn't wait to take Nique to the final destination. I peeped over to see her dancing in the seat. She had the radio blasting, "Whistle While You Twerk." I lowered the music as the song was coming to an end. Rubbing her thigh, I looked over to her and smiled. It's something about falling in love with somebody that just matches you all around. This girl had me whipped. But anyway, I lead her out the car and into the Ritz

Carlton. "Baby, what are we doing here? This is expensive," she said looking at me smiling from ear to ear. "You'll see," I said. Going up to the front desk, I gave my last name and the clerk handed me over the keycard. I walked up to the third floor with Nique holding on to my arms. "Baby, before you go in to see your surprise, I just want to say if your reply is a yes you must kiss me and if it's a no, which I doubt it will be, you get to have this whole room to yourself." Rolling her eyes, she steps behind me. I opened the door and she walked in to see blue painted rose petals and glitter covering the floor, bed, and dressers. Blue raspberry candles lit the floor leading into the bathroom. Candy of all kind covered 91 envelopes for all the days we've been talking for reasons why I loved her.

There were 9 blue, black, and white balloons covering the room. When she turned around, I opened my jacket, so she could see the words on my shirt: "Will you be my girlfriend, Nique?" She jumped in my arms repeating yes Zaddy. I held her as makeup got on my shirt from her crying. Kissing my neck, she slid off me slowly going down pulling on my belt. "Baby no, let me please you first," I said looking into her eyes. She pushed me softly and I landed on the bed. She unbuttoned my shirt, pulled off my pants, and threw it across the room forgetting the candles. We are both goofballs, so we started laughing. She eased off me and blew out the candles. Watching her bend over, I could see her ass jiggle through her black lace panties. Looking over in the drawer, she pulled out the handcuffs and the baby-oil that I was planning to use on her and cuffed me to the bed. She poured some into the cap and dripped it from my neck to my core. My body shook as I felt the coldness hit my body. Nique massaged the oil into my shoulders, down my breast, and around my stomach, softly. I moved my feet upwards so I could position her closer to me. Teasing me, she scooted back and rubbed her breast over mine. Kissing my stomach and upward to my neck, she kissed me more passionately on my lips tugging on my bottom lip. Sliding her tongue over to my ear, I felt a slight tug. Gliding her tongue down my breast, she licked and sucked my nipple while her right hand massaged my other nipple.

"Baby, please let me go," I moaned. She reached over and grabbed more oil and poured it over my center, as she positioned herself right on top of me. Using one hand, caressing my chest and using the other hand sliding in and out of my center, Nique ground her body into mine. Matching her rhythm, I used my lower body strength to grind into her. She reached above me to free the cuffs. I raised up and let one of her titties fall into my mouth, using my free hand I caressed her back. And used my other free hand to rub her cheeks. Wrapping my hands around her waist, I pulled her lower body closer to my lips. I plant kisses on each side of her thighs and licked all around her pussy as I got closer to the center. Sucking on her clit, I reach forward and massaged her breast as she moaned and ground her pussy into my mouth, trailing my tongue to go deeper and deeper. While her legs shook, I felt her juices run down my lip and I licked it up. Placing her on my lap, I sat up and carried her into the bathroom tub filled with soapy, warm water. I turned on the hot water and the jacuzzi sped on high. Nique leaned into me and kissed me passionately, rubbing her hands up my legs.

Sunshine was beaming through the windows landing right across my face. Raising up in the bed, I pulled the sheets up with me to cover my naked body. Nique came from the bathroom with a face mask on. Sliding into the bed, she cuts the TV on. "Go ahead and get fresh, Baby, I ordered us some breakfast," she said. I got out the bed and went into the bedroom to wipe my face, brush my teeth, and shower. Stepping out of the shower, I hear a knock at the door. I heard Nique opening the door. Room Service! I slid into my robe and got into the room, while the guy strolled back out with his cart. While I'm praying over my food, Nique went into the bathroom to wash off her face mask. "So, you're going to start eating without me," Nique said coming back to the bed. "Don't worry, I prayed for us already, go ahead and eat," I said in between bites. She laughed eating on her Belgium Blueberry Waffles. I picked up a piece of bacon and toast and bit into it. Scooting down to the end of the bed, I poked my lips out. Nique kisses me and rubbed her hands through my hair. "Baby let's make a toast," I said as I grabbed my glass. "Cheers to the future us!" we said. Nique clashed her glass against mine. Salute! I took her tray from her and placed it on top of mines. "Baby girl, what you want to do today?" I asked. "Um, Baby, you outdid yourself already. I just really enjoyed spending time with you. I mean unless you had something in mind," she replied. "Yeah actually I do," I smiled. I rolled over on top of her placing my head on her breast, taking in her sweet perfume. She rubbed her hands over my back while watching TV. We chilled in the room, enjoying each other's company for a little while. "Baby, you ready to go?" I ask Nique as I put on my leather jacket. "Yeah, but you never told me where we're going Pookie," she stated. "It's a surprise, beautiful," I smiled.

We left the room and went down to the parking garage. As we got situated in the car, I placed a CD in and drove off into the distance. We stopped at a red light and I pulled out the blindfold I had in my pocket. "Okay baby let me put this blindfold on you because I don't want you to see where we are going," I said placing it over her eyes. "Baby, where are we going? Omg, I'm so nervous," she said leaning back in her seat. I passed by Walmart, Home Depot, and finally, saw the sign that said AMC. I pulled into the closest parking spot available. "Okay, Nique we have arrived. Let me help you take it off," I said placing my hands around her head. She looked around and squinted her beautiful eyes. "Baby, what movie are we going to see?" she yelled out. Laughing, I said, "Nobody's Fool". "How did you know I wanted to see this movie?" she smiled. "Because you have been talking about the trailer of it for the longest. Besides, I listen baby," I said shrugging my shoulders. We got out of the car and held hands. I opened the door for baby girl to go in. We walked up to the clerk to pay for our tickets and food. Walking up the steps, I'm behind Nique as we go all the way to the top. Finding a seat, we got situated and put our phones on vibrate. Nique reached into the popcorn and put it up to my mouth. In the movie, Whoopi Goldberg was bending down like she couldn't hear her daughter through the window. The whole movie theatre cracked up laughing. She and I finished our popcorn and then ate M & M's.

Midway through the movie, it started getting cold. "Baby, it's cold in here," said Nique. I took off my jacket, so she could put it on. She smiles and looked up at me because she knew she was spoiled. I gave her a peck on the cheek and she started rubbing my inner thigh. Now she knew damn well that was one of my "spots". I start swinging my legs back and forth. I looked over at her and she was giggling up a storm. I was blushing hard as hell, trying to keep it together. But you know what they say, "two can play that game". While I looked around to see if anybody was looking, I swallow the gum I was chewing and took my hand and placed it over her lap. I pulled on her skirt and reached my fingers inside her. In no time, she was wet. Her pussy was pulsating around my fingers, as she squirmed in her seat. I knew she wanted me to keep going but soon after I sped up, I pulled my fingers from her and licked them. "Baby, let's go right now," she whispered in my ear. Smiling from ear to ear, I looked into her eyes and said, "Nah, let's finish the movie." I hated telling Nique, no, but it was just too cute to watch her pout. "Please," she whined. "Nope, I promise I'll handle that when we leave baby." She mocked me, and we continued watching the movie. I cracked up laughing in the back of my head. I grabbed my sprite and sipped on the last of it.

The movie came to an end and we gathered our things to head for the door. We got to the car and I turned on the seat massager. Pulling my seatbelt over my body, I looked over at Nique wiping her hair away from her face. She looked so sexy; I could just cuddle with her all night. I drove out into the traffic and made my way down the street. I wanted to take Nique out to eat, but then again, I was a little tired, so I figured we could just order room service. I pulled into the parking garage and ejected the CD I had put in from earlier. Looking over, I saw Nique sleeping. "Baby, wake up," I whispered lightly tapping on her shoulder. She slightly turned to face me and went back to sleep. I stepped out of the car and went to Nique's side and unlocked the door. "Baby, come on we made it back to the hotel," I said. "I'm tired," she pouted turning towards me. Holding her hands out to me, she wrapped her arms and legs around me. I held onto her and closed the door all in one motion, carrying her to our room. I laid her on the bed and gave her a kiss on her forehead. Unzipping my luggage, I pulled out some pajamas. I carried the pajamas into the bathroom, placing them on the side of the sink. Stepping out of my clothes, I plopped down on the toilet. Ring. Ring. I picked up my phone seeing Mommy going across the screen.

"Hey, mama. How was your day?"

"It was good, NaNa. I had quite a few paperwork to do. Patients are doing great, so I feel even better. How was yours?"

"Mama I got to tell…."

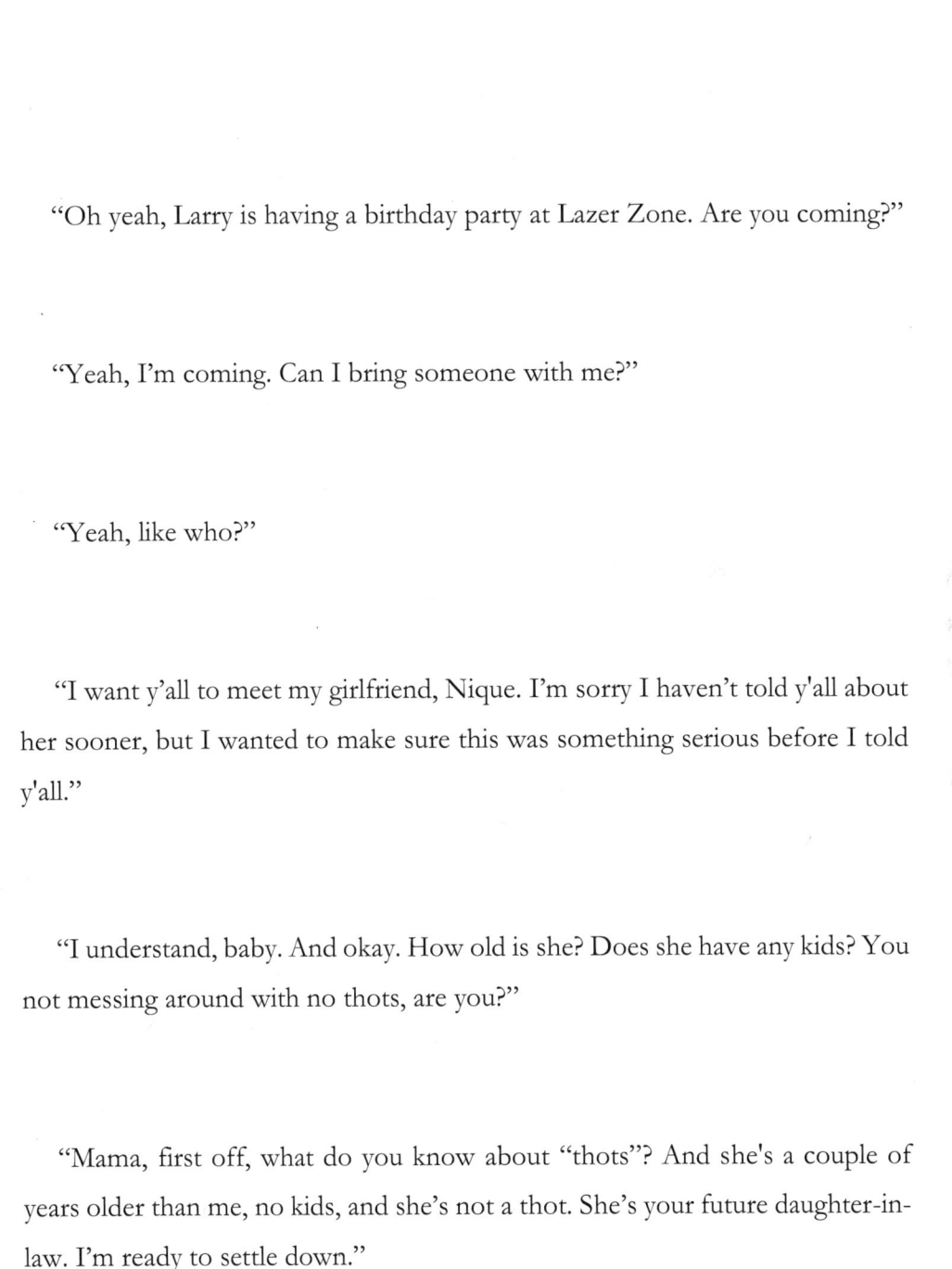

"Oh yeah, Larry is having a birthday party at Lazer Zone. Are you coming?"

"Yeah, I'm coming. Can I bring someone with me?"

"Yeah, like who?"

"I want y'all to meet my girlfriend, Nique. I'm sorry I haven't told y'all about her sooner, but I wanted to make sure this was something serious before I told y'all."

"I understand, baby. And okay. How old is she? Does she have any kids? You not messing around with no thots, are you?"

"Mama, first off, what do you know about "thots"? And she's a couple of years older than me, no kids, and she's not a thot. She's your future daughter-in-law. I'm ready to settle down."

"Alright now. We will see about that. And about time I've been waiting on some grandkids."

"You crazy and alright mama. Send me the address and we will be there."

"Mhmm. Love you, bye."

"Love you too."

I got up from the toilet and grabbed a rag from the closet walking into the shower. Forgetting that Nique was sleeping in the room, I started singing while I washed up. Random thoughts started coming to my head. I wondered what people were going to say about Nique and I being together? I hope they like her. Clearing me of my thoughts, I heard the door crack open. Seductively, Nique peaked her head in and looked me up and down. "Baby can you---" As if Nique was reading my mind, she calmly took off her clothes and joined me in the shower, replying, "Yes, I'll go with you."

Ch10 Family Matters

Nique has been staying at my crib for the last couple of days. She even seemed to be getting along with Princess. I walked into the room and saw her waving Princess's toy in front of her face. I pounced onto the bed and grabbed a pillow and lightly threw it into Nique's direction. She leaped from the floor, grabbed a pillow, and started hitting me with it. I could hear Princess in the back whining as if she was missing out on all the fun. "Princess, are you not going to help your mama out?" I said laughing while Nique bashed me with pillows. I threw a pillow and it missed her and she jumped on top of me. Nique stuck her tongue out and licked my cheek. "Girl stop," I said. She licked me again. I wrapped my hands around her and pulled her panties up through her shorts, giving her a wedgie. "Baby, why did you do that," she whined. We started wrestling around the bed. Baby wrapped her legs around me and pinned my arms to the side, making it hard for me to move. She flicked her tongue back and forth across my lips. I lift my head up to kiss her and she moved back teasing me. "Girl stop teasing me," I said trying to lift up. "Gimme a kiss". Leaning in to give me a kiss, she loosened her grip on me, so I could ease up. Roof! Roof! Princess re-entered the room barking at us and trying to jump on the bed. Nique broke away from the kiss and laid back into bed. "I'm going to give Princess a bath," I told baby girl. "Alright baby, I'm going to make me something to eat. You want something?" she asked. "Yes, whatever you make I'll eat, including you," I said as I picked up Princess off the floor. Nique laughed and made her way into the kitchen.

Carrying Princess into the laundry room, I held her up against my chest to adjust the water. I placed her in the tub, letting the warm water run over her. She's the only dog that I know that likes water so much. She splashes the water with her paws while I poured the shampoo on her back. "Girl be still, little mama," I giggled. I grabbed her brush and went over her fur with it. I rinsed the water off her and as soon as I got ready to cut it off she started barking as if she was telling me to keep it on. I grabbed her favorite customized red and pink doggy towel and pulled her out the tub. "Come on, mama," I whispered. "Baby, yall ready to eat? I fixed our plate, I fixed some food for Princess too and put it in her cage," Nique said. "Awwee you're so sweet baby, thank you," I said placing Princess down. I threw the towel into Princess's laundry bag. Going into the bathroom, I wash and dried my hands. I walked back into the room and saw Nique chomping down on her food. I picked up my plate smelling the freshly cut baked chicken on top of my dirty salad. When we put everything in our salad (mushrooms, pepperoni, eggs, ham meat, turkey meat, tomatoes, lettuce, zucchini, spinach, green onions, cheese, croutons, almonds) that's what we mean by "dirty". And to top it off, Nique made some blue raspberry Kool-Aid. Man, it was hitting the spot.

I felt someone staring at me and looked over to see Nique making faces at me. "Uh-huh caught you," I said. "You were hungry, huh?" she said jokingly. "Hell yeah," I said. "And by the way remind me not to forget Larry's birthday bag before we leave." She shook her head up and down with her mouth full of food. She walked over to the closet to pick out an outfit from her suitcase. "Bae, should I wear this or this?" she asked showing me the outfits. "That one," I said pointing to the one on the right. She decides to stick with it and laid it on the bed and went to the bathroom. I picked up our plates and went into the kitchen to put them in the dishwasher. Princess came running behind me as I entered the room. Sitting down on the floor, she jumped in my lap and turned around laying on her back. Princess loved having her belly rubbed! I picked her up and hugged her. She started licking out her tongue but knew I didn't like being kissed. As I heard the water shut off in the bathroom, I placed her back on the floor. Nique came out of the bathroom, body glistening and dripping water, wrapped in a towel. She glanced in my direction and said, "Drip, Drip!" Man, I cracked up laughing. "Came through dripping," I gasped between laughter.

After gathering myself, I finally got up to go shower. I stripped out of my clothes and turned on the water. I heard the doorknob turn and Nique appeared. "Baby put on some music," I said. Nique turned on her Cardi B playlist. "Knock me down nine times but I get up ten" boomed through the speakers. Nique could not rap to save her life. She left the bathroom and disappeared to wherever she was going, leaving me to dance to the music while I rinsed off. I stepped out the shower and got my towel off the sink. "Look, Bae, I can do the tittie move like Terry Crews," I said poking out my chest with my towel wrapped around my lower waist. Looking in the mirror, Nique turned and faced me laughing. I began playing with my towel teasing her as if I was trying to give her a sneak peek. She came over by me and I danced around her, swinging my towel in the air. Then, Nique's sat on her side of the bed watching me play around. "Baby you better come on before we are late. You should have been ready before me," she said. "I have showered, dressed, and put my makeup on." "Girl we are going to make it. And you don't need makeup anyway," I said. She folded her arms and rolled her eyes at me. "Stop that pouting and come on," I said lacing up my shoes. "Don't forget Lebron's gift, remember?" she smirked. "See, what will I do without you?" I smacked her on the butt. I grabbed his gift and followed her out the door.

I knew exactly where to go so I didn't worry about using the G.P.S. Turning into the main street, I merged into the other lane to get on the highway. I turned off on Exit 7 and rolled into the parking lot. The place was packed out with rows of cars. Baby girl and I went into the building to see where everybody was at. I scoped out my brother shooting balls into a basket. "Baby, they over here," I said reaching out for her hand to follow me. We went over by him and I tapped him on the shoulder dangling his gift bag in front of him. "Wassup sis," he smiles taking the bag from my hands. Grabbing Nique by the waist, I introduced them and we started chatting. I dapped up my brother and asked him where mama was. Looking over to the party room, I saw her eating pizza. We walked over to her and the first thing she said was, "she's pretty." Baby girl and I both said thank you at the same time. "Y'all want some pizza? We still have two boxes left," she said. "No, we're good. We ate before we came. Thanks though," I said. Of course, mama started asking baby girl question after question. "Mama, this is not an interrogation room. Go easy on her," I said. My sister started cracking up laughing like the goofball she is. So, we got to chatting for a bit. Mama was getting the feel of Nique and by the looks of it, they were getting along just well.

We stayed for a few hours spending time with the family, but then I noticed it started to get dark outside. "Alright mama, we're going to get out of here. Nique has to work in the morning," I said hugging my mom. "Okay, yall be careful. And nice meeting you Nique. You're more than welcome to come over anytime," she said smiling. Nique followed behind me through the crowd and entered the car. "Baby you have a nice family," Nique said. "Yeah, for the most part, they don't get on my nerves too much," I chuckled. We got back to the house, took our showers, and crashed. Sleep was definitely calling our names.

The next day Nique had to work. I admired her work ethics to the fullest. I couldn't stop thinking about her. Often, I would daze off dreaming about how our future could go. I snapped out of it thinking of how I was going to plan my day out. I decided to make dinner early so that Nique could have a hot meal when she came home. I knew today was one of her busiest days, so why not treat her to a day of relaxation when she came home. After I fixed dinner, I ate a bowl of cereal with bananas. Going to my living room, I pulled out my yoga mat to exercise and meditate for a bit. Next thing you know, I woke up on the couch. I thought to myself that it must have been one heck of a workout. After gathering myself off the couch, I went and took a shower. I slid into my pajamas and picked up my suitcase from the corner of my room. I pulled out my laptop and went on Google search bar and typed in "houses in Montgomery, Alabama in the 80799 area". Twenty-one houses popped up. I clicked on the first one to view the pictures. Both the outside and inside looked nice, but it didn't have a pool or jacuzzi that I preferred in the back. I scrolled down to look at more of the houses listed. Suddenly, Nique came through the door, sat her suitcase down, kicked off her shoes, and slumped down on the couch.

"Hey, babe. How was your day?"

"It was good. We had a lot of leads today and I sold two houses. How was your day?"

"That's great Nique. I just cleaned and relaxed today. I took the best nap ever. And, oh yeah, I made dinner already if you're hungry."

"Oh, really what did you make?"

them into the room. Returning to the living room, I picked up my laptop and brought it into the room to put it up. I heard the water shut off and I went to the kitchen to fix Nique a plate. Beep! I open the microwave and took out the plate. I put salad on the plate and took it to the room. Baby girl pulled up her shorts. "Can you lotion my legs, bae?" she asked with her puppy dog eyes gleaming. "Of course, baby girl," I said placing her plate on the bed next to us. I took the lotion out of her hand and poured some into my hand and rubbed it around her thigh and down her leg. Grabbing her other leg, I repeated the same motion and by that time she had started eating her food. I grabbed the lotion and put some in my hand rubbing my hands together and massaged her feet. "Baby girl you got some pretty ass feet," I said staring into her eyes. "Thank you, babe. That felt really good." She smiled. I took her plate away and climbed back in the bed. Usually, I would lay on her and go to sleep, but tonight roles changed. Nique got up under the covers and rolled to my side and laid on my chest. "Baby, I love you," she said. "I love you too, baby girl," I said kissing her forehead. I adjusted my arm and rubbed her back as we both drifted off to sleep.

"Babe, when are you going let me meet your parents?"

"I made lasagna and salad. Do you want me to fix you a plate?"

"Yeah, I'm so tired though."

"Babe I think it's time we take things to the next level and start look houses. I mean we already stay together and you met my peoples."

"Yeah, I agree. We can start looking sometime soon. But baby I'm tir just ready to eat and get some sleep."

"Okay baby girl. I'm so excited we're on the same page. I really feel like are falling into place. I just can't wait to…" I say as I look over and saw knocked out. I placed my laptop on the sofa and went into the bathroom t Nique some water. Pouring some body wash and Epsom salt in the wa turned the nozzle and shut it off. Ring! Ring! Nique's phone woke her u her sleep and she looked at it and declines the call reading SCAM LIK "Babe, I ran you some bath water," I told her as she got up. She kisses me went into the bedroom. I walk over to get her suitcase and heels and bro

"Umm, babe you know how my mama is. She doesn't accept the fact that I'm a lesbian."

"I understand Nique, but I would like to at least try. I want to ask your father for his blessings in marrying you. And I promise I'll be right there by your side if anything goes left."

"Yeah, I know you always have me, baby. But I really don't think it's a good idea."

"I understand Nique. Whenever you're ready, I'll be right here."

"It's like I really want to, but I don't think you understand how much she hates gay people. When she found out I liked girls she verbally and emotionally abused me. She called me all kind of malicious names you cannot begin to think of…faggot, slut, whore, girl freak, carpet eater, cherry popper, cootie licker, a bitch, etc. She would look at me as if I had a disease that was contagious, and she was afraid to catch it. Being around her was tearing our relationship apart. She always wondered who I was on the phone with and if it was a girl she would pass by my room and just stare at me, disgustingly. She would treat me as if I was the stepchild she never wanted. I can't control how I feel about another human being. If I could, I wouldn't choose this life."

Nique broke down crying and started hitting herself uncontrollably. I ran over to her and grabbed her hands and wrapped them around me, letting her cry into my chest. I rubbed her back as she let it all out. Seeing her break down like that really broke my heart. I really wanted to go over to her parent's house and ask them what was up. But I had to stay strong for baby girl. The heat radiating from her felt so thick I thought she was going to pass out. I brought her over to the couch and she sat on my lap with her hands covering her face buried in my chest. "Baby girl, look at me," I said sternly. "You are beautiful. God still loves you; I love you, and other people do too. We will get through this together. I promise you don't have to deal with this alone. I'm right here. I won't leave you." Nique slowly lifted her head up and wiped her face from the stream of tears. Her bright brown eyes that looked as if they were bleeding from all the crying were now looking right into mine. I could tell her mind was racing and by the looks of her shirt, her heart look liked it was about to drop right in my lap. As if she couldn't speak above a whisper, she grabbed my hands and kissed it and began to say, "Diana I love you so much. I wouldn't trade this relationship for anything in the world. I'm sorry I acted out like that. But it's like I was having flashbacks of how it was living with my mom and how she treated me and I lost it." "Baby girl you don't have to apologize. I understand how you feel and know I'm always here for you," I said as a tear came down my face, "I love you too." She wiped my face and hugged me for what felt like an eternity. It was quiet for some minutes until Nique broke the silence. She suggested that we take a shower together and have a movie night.

We went into the bathroom and started stripping off our clothes. I got in first and she followed. I lathered the soap and began washing my body. Baby girl did the same thing and then she gave me her rag to wash her back and I gave her mine to do the same. Now it was time to rinse off and she had the water on high, I thought my ass cheeks were going to fall off. Trying to put the soap back up, I dropped it and it fell closer to Nique. "Oops, I dropped the soap," I said laughingly. Nique bent over and picked it up giving me a good view. I opened the shower door and stepped out, getting out towels for us to dry off. I really felt like going commando, so I dried off and put on my robe. Reaching for my phone, I called up Pizza Hut and ordered two Large Supreme Pizzas, 12-pieces of buffalo wings, and an order of cinnamon sticks. They told me my order would arrive in 20 minutes. "Bae, why are you not putting on clothes?" Nique laughingly asked me. "I don't know. I just feel like being naked. Why? You can't handle all this caramel being next to you?" I tease laying in the bed next to her while she put on her clothes. "Girl whatever, before I have you tapping out like you did yesterday," she smirked. "Mhm ok," I said grinning and flipping through the channel to see what movies were playing. I passed her the remote because I couldn't find anything interesting.

As soon as I got up to get something to drink from the kitchen the doorbell rang. Reaching for my wallet, I looked over and saw baby pulling out some money. "I got it, NaNa," she said. She walked over to give the man the money while I watched from afar to make sure she was okay. Shutting the door, Nique came back into the room and placed the box in between us. She took a slice of pizza and waved it in front of my face. I acted as if I was going to take a bite and ended up taking the whole pizza out of her hand. "Big mouth head ass," she joked. "Gotta be quicker than that," I laughed trying to swallow the pizza at the same time. I stuck a chicken wing in my mouth eating it down to the bone. We started hearing Princess barking in her cage. She was definitely missing out, but the wings were too hot for her to handle, for sure. Nique and I made small talk while finishing up our food. I took the boxes and sat them on the kitchen counter. I crawled back into bed and turned the TV to the R&B music station. "Babe, you know what? I will not let my mama keep having power over me. I'm ready to face her," she said looking into my eyes. "Are you sure, baby girl?" I asked. "Yes, I'm very sure. Now let's get some sleep," she said turning over to cut the lamp off on her side of the bed. Scooting closer to her, I wrap my arm around her locking my hands into hers. I kissed her shoulder and closed my eyes and drifted off to sleep.

Waking up, I looked over at the time and saw it was nearing one o'clock. Princess waddles over to my side of the bed and tried to jump on the bed. I dangled my hand off the bed and pat her on the head. "Did you get some good sleep?" Nique asked. "I was trying to wake you up to see if you wanted some breakfast, but you were knocked out. Raising up in the bed, I replied, "Yeah, I guess I did. We still going to your parents?" "Yeah, I've dressed already. And if you want to, we can stop to get something to eat cause I'm hungry again." "Alright, let me get dressed," I said stretching while going into the closet. I picked out my ripped blue jean pants and Givenchy shirt and placed them on the bed. I took my shower and dried off, going into the room to put on my clothes. I slipped my hair into a ponytail and Nique came in between my legs with her hands on my shoulders. I grabbed her by the waist and she dramatically fell on top of me. "Baby come on let's go. I'm hungry," I said. "Nope, give me kiss first," she teased. Smooch! I gave her kisses and she stood back up, proceeding to leave the room. I followed her out the door and headed to the car.

We decided to grab a bite to eat at Taco Bell. I pulled into the driveway and ordered the Supreme Taco meal and baby girl a Mexican Pizza Taco meal. We waited for about ten minutes and received our food. I passed Nique the food to make sure we had everything. She gave me back my food and I placed it in my lap, picking it up to take a bite every now and then. We finally made it up to her parent's house. Putting the car in park, I licked my lips to remove the crumbs. I checked the mirror to see if any food was in my teeth. Nique opened her door and got out. I met her in front of the car. "You ready?" I assured her. Nodding her head forward, she grabbed my hand and continued to walk ahead. Nique pushed her finger against the doorbell. Her father opened the arm and waved for us to come in. Following behind Nique, I looked around the house at my surroundings. Her father yelled out for her mother to meet us in the living room.

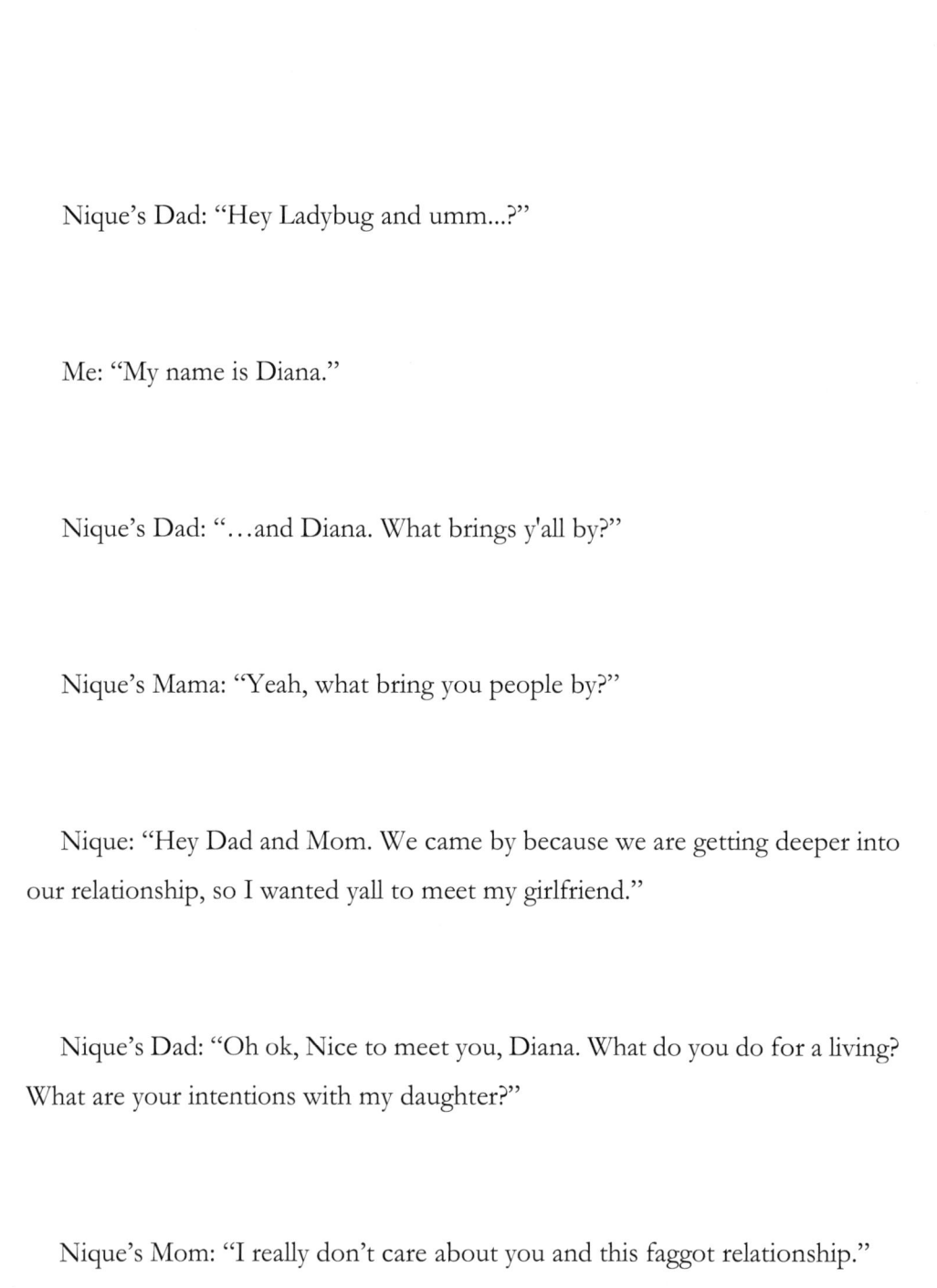

Nique's Dad: "Hey Ladybug and umm...?"

Me: "My name is Diana."

Nique's Dad: "...and Diana. What brings y'all by?"

Nique's Mama: "Yeah, what bring you people by?"

Nique: "Hey Dad and Mom. We came by because we are getting deeper into our relationship, so I wanted yall to meet my girlfriend."

Nique's Dad: "Oh ok, Nice to meet you, Diana. What do you do for a living? What are your intentions with my daughter?"

Nique's Mom: "I really don't care about you and this faggot relationship."

Nique's Dad: "Apologize to Diana right now! And don't you ever disrespect our daughter and her girlfriend like that. Now you have been saying stuff for too long. And quite frankly, I'm tired of it."

Nique's Mom: "I'm not apologizing for anything. I don't approve of our daughter being gay. She already knows how I feel about the whole situation. She or no one else will make me change my views."

Nique's Dad: "You know what I'll deal with you later. Go ahead and go do whatever you were getting ready to do."

Me: "As I was getting ready to say earlier, my name is Diana and I own a clothing store and I am CEO of Tween Queen Ministry Empowering Sisterhood. Another reason why we're here is that I wanted to see if I could get your approval in marrying your daughter."

Nique's Dad: "I am very flattered that you want to get my approval, but all I have to say is yes! Treat my daughter right and we won't have any problems. It looks like you make my daughter very happy. So happy, it brings tears to my eyes seeing her glow like this. I apologize for her mother's behavior and if you both need anything you're always welcome to give me a call."

Nique: "Awwe, don't cry daddy. Thank you for being supportive and loving me through it all. I just wish she (her mother) would at least try to get along."

Me: "Thank you for your blessings, sir. It really means a lot to me. I promise that I will continue to treat your daughter like the Queen she is."

Nique's Dad: "Yall are welcome anytime. Nique, I love you. I want nothing but the best for you. I will always be here for you no matter what."

Nique got up to hug her dad. Pulling from the hug, I saw her father wipe his eyes. Following behind him, he led us out the door. We got inside the car and watched as her father waved from the porch. I pulled out the driveway and out into the street that curved into the main road. "Babe, I'm very proud of you for holding it together when my mama called you out of your name," Nique said rubbing my hand. I look over at her and said, "I'm proud of you too, love. You really held your ground. I can't wait until we start planning for the wedding."

"Me too, babe," she said calmly leaning back into her seat. I pulled up at the apartment and we went in to unwind. Baby girl went into the bathroom, while I took off my jacket and shoes. Cutting on the TV, I flipped through the channels and suddenly blacked out. Rubbing the crust out of my eyes, I realized that I must've fallen asleep on Nique last night because looking down under the cover I saw I still had the same clothes on from yesterday. I peeped over at Nique and saw that she was knocked out in the fetal position. I eased out of the bed and went into the bathroom to take a shower and do the rest of my morning hygiene. Going into my closet, I threw on a shirt and some shorts. Before I left, I wrote a love letter to express my love for her, to express how I felt about her, and to express how much I wanted her to stay by my side and left it on my side of the bed. Making sure not to wake up Princess, I grabbed my keys and wallet and headed out the door.

The first stop I made was to Starbucks and ordered the largest Vanilla Iced Coffee. After that, I went to the shop to check on the status of things. Pulling up into the parking lot, I saw that the sign was finally up. I stepped out of the car and walked over to the construction workers. Walking in the shop, I glanced around to see the painting finished and the lights installed. Men were bringing in furniture into my office and the security room. "Where do you want this frame to go?" one of the crewmen asked. "Right over here to the right behind that rack," I said pointing behind him. I went into my office and sat down in the black leather swivel chair I ordered off Amazon. Dazing out, I visioned the final touches of the shop, having a huge grand opening, and everybody having a good time. Snapping out of it, I remembered that I needed to go get supplies out of my car. I went out to my car and took out the decorations and supplies to bring back into the office. I stayed around for a couple of hours to make sure everything was in order and progress was being made. Satisfied with a great job everyone was doing, I went home to check on Nique.

"Baby girl, I'm home," I yelled out going into the kitchen grabbing a bottle of water. I guess she didn't hear me because I didn't hear a reply back. The farther I entered the bedroom, the louder the music was getting. I opened the closet door to see Nique dancing with one of my shirts on looking as if it was stuffed in the middle. "Baby girl what are you doing?" I laughed. She jumped and took the pillow from underneath her clothes, hiding it from behind her back. "Umm nothing," she said looking innocent. "So, what's behind your back then?" I asked. She plopped down on the floor and sat on it. "NaNa I want a baby." She said looking at me with the puppy dog face. I kneeled beside her figuring that this was going to be a long conservation.

"I mean we love each other. We're always talking about our future together. It's not like we are financially hurting."

"I love you with everything in me, baby girl. But you know we've been busy, Babe. Having a baby in the mix would add more stress on us. Let's wait until after the building gets finished and we have some employees first. Besides, I love that it's just us right now."

"I understand we've been busy. But Bae by the time the baby gets here all those things should be done. We could get a babysitter and still go to work."

"Now you know how I feel about babysitters. And on the other hand, we still have time. We haven't gone out and traveled like I wanted to, yet. Not to mention, we haven't got married yet. You must be having baby fever?"

"Yeah, I mean everybody else getting pregnant, having kids, and starting families. And I want the same thing for us. We will be great parents, especially you. I see how you interact with your brothers and sister."

"Babe, we will have a family someday. But just because everybody having theirs now doesn't mean we have to have one right now. And I know we will make great parents someday. As of right now, let's continue to love each other, have fun, and build with each other so our future princess or prince doesn't have to worry about anything," I said calmly grasping her chin and giving her a kiss on the cheek. "Well let's have some fun right now like what you said in that love letter," she said climbing on top of me.

Ch11 For Better or Worse

Rolling over to wrap my arms around Nique, I woke up to see the other side of the bed was empty. Rubbing my eyes, I looked around to see signs of her leaving and spotted a note on the dresser. I walked over and picked up the note that read: "Hey, sexy, you looked so peaceful in your sleep, I didn't want to wake you. My job called so I went ahead and went in early. I have a present for you. And, by the way, feed Princess, she was sleep when I left." I staggered over to where Princess was and saw a big shiny gift bag. Slowly picking up the bag, I peeked inside to see what was in it without waking up Princess. I walked back to my room, sat down on the edge of the bed, and pulled out the box. Blushing, I pulled out the Jordan Legacy 312's. I reached over on the nightstand to pick up my phone and to send Nique a text: "Hey beautiful, I hope you're having a good day at work. Thank you for the shoes. I love you." With the quickness, she texted back, "You are welcome baby. And meet me at 313 Michigan Blvd., around two o'clock." I replied and went into the bathroom to do my morning hygiene. Walking over to the kitchen, I grabbed a bowl and spoon out of the cabinet and got the milk out of the refrigerator. I poured some frosted flakes and milk into the bowl. I cleaned my stuff up and went back into the room and turned on the radio. I finished up my bowl of cereal and placed it on my nightstand.

"Princess let's get your day started," I said. Roof! Roof! I let her out of the cage and opened the back door, so she could use it. She ran over to a bush in the corner and lift her leg up. "Good girl, mamas," I said. She came back running and I held out my hand so she could retrieve her treat. I got her doggy bowl and put some water in it and then placed some treats in the other. Running over to her water bowl, she happily started lapping it up. I went back into my room and saw that it was nearing 12:30 and made my bed up. Looking in the hallway closet, I pulled out the vacuum and began to use it over the carpet. Then, I sprinkled the lavender carpet freshener over the carpet. I quickly hopped in the shower and lathered my body. As I dried off, I looked through my closet to see what outfit would match the shoes Nique bought for me. Bingo! I found the perfect outfit. I pulled the clothes off the hanger and laid them on the bed. Pulling out the cherry blossom lotion, I spread it over my arms and legs. Then, I put on my clothes and most importantly my shoes. Grabbing my wallet, keys, and phone, I checked to make sure Princess was good before leaving the house.

I pulled out of the parking garage and rolled slowly into the street. Tapping on my touchscreen, I looked for the G.P.S and typed in the address. Searching for the auxiliary cord, I connected it to my phone and turned the volume on high. The sun radiated through the window even with the visor in place. Therefore, I took my shades from the eyeglass case and put them on. Pulling up into the driveway, I saw Nique getting out her car with paperwork in her hand. I put the car in park and walked over to her to see what we were doing here. "Hey baby, I liked those shoes you have on and thanks for coming over. I wanted to see if you could do some work in this backyard for my client. But since I haven't looked over the houses yet and we have been busy lately, I thought maybe this was the perfect time to do so. You mind doing that with me?" she asked. "Sure thing baby, thanks for picking them out. And what kind of work do they need to be done in their backyard?" I asked. "The couple wanted a fence in the backyard, enough for two dogs to run around and play," she said. "Alright, bet. I'm sure I can get Christopher to help me with that," I said.

Standing in the middle of the living room, we scoped out the shiny wooden floors, the sparkling four-tier chandelier, and the stone fireplace. We walked over to the stainless kitchen with a big open space. There was a lot of cabinet space, a double-jointed sink, and a French door refrigerator. Walking over to the hallway, I noticed a door somewhat open and peeped my head on the inside. I flickered the light on the wall and saw that it was a half bathroom suitable for guests. We looked through some rooms and finally got down to the last room---the master bedroom. "Dang babe, you helped them pick out a nice house," I said. "You know how I do it, baby," she smirked. Looking around the spacious room, I saw a wooden closet door. Nique walked in front of me revealing the walk-in closet. "Man, babe, I can't wait until we find a good house like this," I said grabbing her by the waist, kissing her on her forehead. "We will baby. Trust me," she said pulling me over to what looked like another closet.

Surprisingly, it was his and hers double-sink bathroom. I hugged Nique from behind, kissed the inside of her neck. I pulled her around and set her up on top of the sink. Rubbing my hands up her sides, I sucked all over her neck. Tilting her head back, she moaned in my ear. Getting ready to take my shirt off, Nique pulled it down. "Umm no babe, we can't do this here," she laughed. "Damn, you right," I chuckled. "Sorry I kind of got carried away." "Yeah, we both did," she blushed, "Help me zip my dress up, please." I zipped it up and adjusted my clothes. As if nothing happened, we went back up the hallway so we could finish checking out the rest of the house. Walking out to the patio, the sun was glaring right in my face. There were a nice size pool and jacuzzi surrounded by yards of very freshly cut, green grass. Pointing over to the far corner, I suggested, "Nique, maybe that would be a good area for the fence to go up. It's enough space for the dogs to run around and also be away from the pooling area." "I think the clients would love that idea babe," she smiled. "Now, let's go back in." I followed her back into the house through the Fiber French patio doors. Rubbing my stomach, I started thinking about how hungry I was. I was about to ask Nique what she had a taste for until I saw that she looked like she was searching for something with her face all scrunched up.

"Babe, can you hand me the papers over there. I must've forgotten about them when we were in the kitchen." She said. I walked over to the table in the living room and picked up the clipboard. Sneaking a glance over it, I saw that it has Nique's signature and today's date. "Ummm why is this house signed in your name baby," puzzled I said walking back over to her. "Because this is ours,

Baby," she smiled dangling the keys in the air. "Man, this is not real. Are you serious?" I asked. "Yes, I am serious. I know we have been talking a lot about houses and it seems like we were having a hard time finding one, but when I saw this one I figured it was the one, she said. Crying and running towards her, I picked her up and spun her around all in one motion. I placed her back on her feet and just blatantly stared at her. I couldn't believe that I was really experiencing life with the love of my life. "So, go ahead and sign these papers," she said handing me back the clipboard. I signed my name as I had just received the biggest check, smiling from ear to ear. Nique locked up the house and we raced each other home.

"Why you ain't wash these dishes? You had most of them in there."

"I can wash them when I get ready."

"You should've washed them. It's a pile of damn dishes in there. You so fucking lazy."

"Bruh, Ima wash the dishes. You ain't got to yell at me like you my mama or something."

"So when you gone wash the fucking dishes then? And don't nobody want to be your mama. If you would do what the fuck you need to do. Then, we wouldn't be having this damn discussion."

"Look leave me the fuck alone. I told you Ima wash the dishes."

"Shut up talking to me. And how about you sleep on the couch tonight since you want to act fucking retarded."

"Yeah ok, whatever."

I don't know what came over her and why she was acting all stank. But she was really ruining my mood. Like, I know things should be kept in order, but she didn't have to come at me like that. I got up from the couch and walked into the bathroom to shower. Ignoring her gaze, I put on my pajamas and went back to the living room. I cut on the TV and turned to Pandora. I walked over to the kitchen and washed the dishes that were in the sink. After that, I went back to the couch and scrolled to the movie "Bird Box". I couldn't help but think about the argument Nique and I had earlier, so I went into the bedroom. As soon as I came in, she switched over to her side of the bed. I sat up in the bed and patted her on her arm to see if she would turn back my way. She didn't budge.

"Baby girl sit up, please. We need to talk and we not about to go to bed mad at each other."

"Oh, so now you want to talk."

"We are not about to argue again. Just listen."

"Alright. I'm listening. What?"

"I don't like the way you went off on me. I understand that we have house duties. But if I tell you that I'm gone do something then I will do it."

"Well, I guess I did come off kind of hard. But please just help out more. And do you forgive me for jumping down your throat?"

"I will help out more, baby girl. And I forgive you for going loco on me."

She leaned in and got on top of me and French kissed me. Slightly pushing me back, she licked down my neck. Leaving hickies around my breast, she sucked my nipples. Going farther down, disappearing underneath the covers, she kissed and licked all over my pussy.

Today was moving day and we had all our boxes packed and ready to go. Baby Girl and I both are driving separate U-hauls to the new home. I pulled into the driveway with her tagging along behind me. I hopped out, pulling the lever in the back, to retrieve the boxes. Nique came over and pulled a box out. Walking behind her, I reached for the keys in my pocket to unlock the door. We walk in and placed the boxes in the living room. That lasted for a few hours and then, we decided that we would go get some ice cream. She pulled up into Sonic's cubicle and parked the car. Looking at the screen, she looked to see what she wanted. I already knew what I wanted, the Chocolate Oreo Shake. She pressed the button and told the lady our order. As we waited for the lady, we discussed how we wanted to set up the living room and master room. The lady skated over to the car and Nique handed her the money. Nique passed me my shake and straw. I was jealous Nique's had two cherries in hers. We switched cups and tasted each other shakes. I faked like I was going to eat her cherry and she pouted at me.

Giving her back her shake, I leaned back in my seat. I turned the radio on and turned the volume on low. Baby girl had her legs stretched out over me. Rubbing her legs, I sneakily brought up her ring size. Before getting too cozy, we made our way back to the house. It seemed like I was living in a fairytale. Here I was at a young age, owning my first home, my career was taking off, and had a beautiful woman by my side that I wanted to spend the rest of my life with. We went into the bathroom and took a shower. Since we are getting all new furniture, we didn't have our bed yet. I got the electronic blow-up mattress out one of the boxes and turned it on. Princess slept through the noise in her bed. Nique and I watched Netflix until we fell asleep.

Weeks went by and we were getting really comfortable with the house. Picking up my phone, I saw "Baby Girl" flashing across my screen. I answered the phone, hearing loud sniffles in the background. "Baby, are you crying? What's wrong?" I asked. "You're not going to believe what just happened?" Nique sobbed. "What's that? Do you need me to come where you are?" I said puzzled as to what she was about to say next. "No, you don't need to come. And they fired me today, talking about they are cutting down on workers," she stated. "What am I supposed to do? That job was my everything." "Everything is going to be okay. The bills are paid up. We will figure something out, baby girl. Are you on your way home?" I asked. She told me she was on her way and I hung up the phone. I couldn't believe they played Nique like that. She came to work on time, she stayed over when needed, and her clients loved her, but then again maybe it's for the best. One thing for sure, I wasn't worried about anything. I knew that God was going to make sure things got done one way or another. Kneeling beside the bed, I got on my knees and prayed, specifically for baby girl. Getting up, I turned around to see baby girl standing in the door. She smiled faintly and walked over to me and I embraced her with a hug. Both of us sat at the side of the bed and we discussed what our plan was for baby girl moving forward and our financial budget. I liked the plan that we came up with because it meant that Nique got to stay home more. No more being worried about a boss being over her. While she was getting ready for movie night, I went into the kitchen and cut up some fruit. I placed the fruit on the tray and put some sugar in a bowl next to it.

Nique came out of the bathroom in her towel and went over to her dresser. She picked up her strawberry scented oil and sat down on the bed. I placed the fruit on the side of the nightstand. Reaching for the body oil, I asked, "may I?" She nodded her head and stretched the towel across the bed and laid on her stomach. I poured the oil in my hand and started rubbing it on her shoulders, slowly pressing down her back, and making my way down her jiggly butt. I poured more oil into my hand, caressed her booty, and strolled slowly down her legs. "Baby, I love you." She stayed turning over. Hovering over her and pressing my hands on the side of her, I kissed her forehead, her nose, and her plump lips. I passed her a robe and laid in the bed next to her and held the fruit tray. Love & Basketball was playing on the TV, so we settled for that. Nique took a strawberry, dipped it in the sugar, and fed it to me. We finished up the fruit and the movie were still playing. Baby girl snuggled up against me and started playing on her phone. I could tell she was getting sleepy because she was rubbing her eyes. I waited until she got into a deep sleep and I grabbed my phone on the nightstand. Flipping through my phone, I looked up Tiffany & Co. I scrolled down looking at all the beautiful rings. Boom! I finally found "the one" that I knew baby-girl was going to like. I took a screenshot of it. After that I looked up the nail shop my sister went to and saved the number in my phone. I texted my homegirl Breanna and asked her how much she would charge for a full-face.

After doing all that, I was sleepy and adjusted Nique on my chest so I could get comfortable. Smelling something cooking, I woke up from my sleep. I looked over at the time and saw that it was 11:30. I thought to myself like dang, the next day came by fast. Snapping out of the daze, I went to brush my teeth and wash my face. After that, I sneakily tiptoed in the kitchen wrapped my hands around baby girl, kissing the inside of her neck. She giggled, "Baby, come on stop. I'm trying to cook." I grabbed two glasses out the cabinet, rinsed them out, and put some ice and orange juice in it. Nique turned off the burner and fixed our plate. We're sat at the barstool eating on bacon, eggs, and pancakes. Finishing up my plate of food, I looked at Nique still chomping down on hers. "Baby girl my family is having a dinner at Briquettes and invited us, so I scheduled a nail, toes, and eyebrow appointment for you, and Breanna is coming by to do your makeup." I smiled sneakily. "And you figured I was going to go?" she smirked. "Because I'm going," I said. "What am I going to wear?" she asks. "I got you covered. Don't worry about it," I assured her. I kissed her forehead and walked into our office room. I could feel her looking at me as if I had something up my sleeve. I was trying so hard to play it cool.

A couple minutes later I heard, "Baby, I'm gone." I yelled back to her saying, "Okay, love you. Have a good day." Finally! Now that she's gone, I can finish planning what I was about to do. First, I called my family and asked if they could meet me at Briquettes around eight. They agreed. I hung up from them and called Nique's dad to see if he could come. He told me that he would and he'll just leave his wife at home. I called up Christopher to tell him the big news and of course, he had jokes. We talked and joked for a little bit then I hung up. Setting the alarm to the house, I grabbed my keys and headed for my car. The first stop I made was to Party City to buy some balloons. The second stop was to Flowerama to get flowers that last up for seven years. Next stop was Walmart where I pretty much got everything else that I needed! Last stop was the mall. I walked inside the Gucci store and saw this beautiful red and gold dress. I looked at the tag and it read $2,700. I took the dress off the rack and looked around to see if they had some red-bottom heels. Sparkling in the corner of my eye, I found the perfect pair of shoes to go with the dress. I picked up the shoes and checked to see if they were the right size. Walking over to the cashier, I placed the items on the counter and got my wallet out of my pocket. I then went down to Tiffany & Co's to pick up my last items. Feeling happy about how I thought today would go, I started blushing all over again with butterflies in my stomach. Now the only thing left to figure out was how I would take all this stuff in the house without

Nique noticing? Hmmm. I figured I would just sneak it in the movie room because she rarely went in there. I was blasting twerk music all the way to the house. Making sure baby girl was nowhere in sight, I texted Breanna to see where Nique was at. Thank God she was in the bathroom, so the coast was clear! I hurried and placed the items in the movie room and quietly shut the door behind me. "Heyyy, what's up y'all?" I said coming in the room with Nique's outfit. Nique popped her head out of the bathroom and smiled at me. Nique came over to me, "Babe you got something for me?" "Yep, I sure do. Here you go," I said. She unwrapped the box and pulled out the shoes. I was glad to see she wasn't sad anymore over losing her job because better days were ahead. She opened the bag and held the dress up to her body. Jumping up into my arms, I held her as she planted kisses all over my face. "Alright babe, I love you too. Now get your make-up done," I smiled slapping her on the butt. "Where my gifts at?" Breanna asked. "At the store," I laughed. "I got your money though for the make-up." I passed her sixty dollars and she stuck it in her breast.

    I went into the bathroom and peeled from my clothes. Stepping under the showerhead, I let the warm water race down my body. I lathered up my body and rinsed off. Reaching for my towel, I listened through the door to see if Breanna was still there. Didn't hear a thing so I stepped out from behind the door and I stood there in awe. Nique was drop-dead gorgeous, better than the models straight off the runway. "You like my outfit babe?" she snapped me out of the daze. "I love it babe. You wear it beautifully," I winked. Going over to my side of the closet, I looked through my clothes to find something to match

Nique. That's when my eyes landed on this off-white red designer shirt and my black cut up jeans. Looking through my shoes, I picked up my red, black, and gold Gucci shoes I had never worn. I went back out to the bedroom and looked on my dresser to pick out the perfume I wanted to wear. "Baby you are looking sexy," Nique whispered in my ear. "Thank you, baby girl. Ready to go?" I asked pulling my glasses off the dresser, turning to give her a peck on the lips. And just like that we were on our way to the "family dinner". Baby girl scrolled to Snapchat waving the phone in my face saying, "look at Zaddy y'all".

I found us a parking spot closer to the door. Going around to Nique's spot, I helped her out the car. Taking her arm into mine as if we were going to a ball, I walked through the doors and checked for familiar faces. That's when I spotted Nique's dad waving at me. I walked over to the table and pulled out Nique's chair. We greeted everybody and made small talk. Conversations were flowing, the vibes were just right, and everybody was having a good time getting to know one another. The waiter came by and rolled over everybody drinks. I'm surprised baby girl didn't suspect anything. And that's when the waiter came over with the roses I bought earlier. "Here's a special delivery for Nique," he said. She smiles and reached for the flowers. While she sniffed them, I snapped up some off-guard pictures. Reading the card, Nique dabbed her eyes to keep from crying. "Baby these are beautiful. You shouldn't have." She smiles at me. "All for my baby. I had to," I said. Everybody meals were being brought out minute by minute. The waiter from earlier came back out again and placed three boxes in front of Nique. She gasped, placing both of her hands over her mouth. Opening the first box, she pulled out a bracelet, the second box she opened was a necklace, and the final box was earrings. "OMG baby," she exclaimed looking over at me. "You must have spent a fortune on me. I can't believe you--- "You deserve it, baby girl. I told you I would always treat you like the Queen you are," I smiled. The waiter came out and brought Nique and I plate to the table. Everybody was eating their food and conversing here and there. Digging in my coat pocket, I pulled out a small rainbow box. I took Nique's hand into mine and got down on one knee. Looking into her eyes, I began to tell her how I was feeling. "Baby girl when I first saw you at Lakeside Mall, I could not get you out of my mind. I really didn't believe in love at first sight until I met you. You're like the Ying to my Yang and you know how I feel about my Ying Yang Twins. Lol. When I thought about my future, I couldn't picture it without you. I can't sleep without you in the bed next to me. My day goes blah when you are not by my side. I cannot even imagine a life without you. I want to continue to conquer the world with you. So instead of feeling like that, can you make me the happiest woman in the world and marry me and become Mrs. Nique Naomi Baker-Boatwright?

Final Thoughts

In the beginning of 4th grade is when my writing journey began. It started when my teacher introduced us to the four types of writing which was expository, persuasive, narrative, and descriptive. The way she explained it was not sticking to me. Moving over to 5th grade, everything was clicking in when my new teacher explained it. "Girl, you have a gift. You started off not getting it and now look at you," she said. I was turning in 4+ papers left on right. From then on, I was in love with writing. I would write various types of poems and stories.

After a while, school and life started taking a toll so I stopped writing. Suddenly I became homeless and it pushed me to start back writing. I couldn't express myself to others, so I figured the only way to get the pain out of me was to write it. It was a special connection between me and a pen and paper. It was like medicine to the heart for me.

Writing this book was a challenge for me. Not because it was hard, but because I wondered how people would perceive it. How would people view me? Would I get backlash from it? What if no one cared to read it? Getting rid of the fear I was holding on to, I kept reminding myself to shake it off. I knew that if I only reached one person then I did a job well done. Then I realized, it's not about me or what others may think. It's about touching the lives of young girls, letting them know that they can do or be anything they want in life, letting them know that they can get through any obstacle that tries to hinder them, letting them know that they don't have to live by society's rules, and giving them hope that better days are ahead. It is to bring awareness to the situations that young girls don't want to talk about because they feel like they're misunderstood or simply scared to have a voice.

It was also very fun writing my very first book. I enjoyed the learning process of publishing this book and the wonderful connections I made. Writing this book actually served as a part of my healing process for me. A lot of the things Diana went through I went through, although names and relationship references have been altered. A part of telling a story is being able to accept your circumstances and tell your own story. I had to come to grips that even though I have been through so much, I have control of where my destiny lies. Same as the young lady that is reading this right now. Hold onto your crown, love!

"What lies between you and your destiny is the STEPS you take."

~Saniyah Baker-Boatwright

About the Author

Saniyah Baker-Boatwright is a freelance writer from Detroit, Michigan, but currently resides in Alabama. She is a CEO and Founder of Tween Queen Empowering Sisterhood with Saniyah Diane. Through her organization, she mentors girls age thirteen to nineteen in becoming the women they are destined to be. She's also a Project Admin Assistant at Dai Baker Creative Group LLC, handling majority of the business aspects. With an Advanced Honors Diploma, she graduated Murphy High School with a 4.2 grade point average. In her spare time, she enjoys listening to music, traveling, mentoring, reading, and journaling. For inquires, she can be contacted through the following:

Email: sbbthebaoat@gmail.com

Facebook: https://www.facebook.com/SBBTheBaOAT/

Instagram: @sbbthebaoat

Twitter: @SBaoat